"I'm Going To Be A Single Mom."

Nick sat back in his seat, looking stunned. "How? Who's going to be the father?"

"I'm going to use a donor."

After a long moment of silence, Nick said, "You really want to do it. Have a baby, I mean."

"I really do."

"What if I had a better way? For both of us."

Both of them? She failed to see how her plan to have a baby could in any way benefit him. "I'm not sure what you mean."

"I know the perfect man to be the father of your baby. Someone who would actually be around. Someone willing to take financial responsibility for the rest of the baby's life."

Whoever this so-called perfect man was, he sounded too good to be true. "Oh, yeah?" she said. "Who?"

He leaned forward, his dark eyes serious. "Me."

Dear Reader,

Welcome to my new series, The Caroselli Inheritance! And the next installment of my "Getting to know Michelle" reader letters.

Spring has always been my favorite time of year. For the past twenty-two years, since we bought our first house, it's meant that it's time to plant the vegetable garden. I've had many hobbies over the years—drawing, painting, crafts, crochet—but by far my favorite and most consistent is gardening.

First I have to decide what to plant. Around the middle of February I make a list of what we'll need for the year, then I fire up the lights in the greenhouse in my basement, run to English Gardens for seeds and soil, and get to work. I've been starting my own plants for several years now, although I used to buy them, and though I know it sounds a little silly, each year it continues to amaze me to watch the tender little seedlings sprout, then grow into thriving plants.

Strangely enough, the actual planting is my least favorite part, and I can't say I'm thrilled picking weeds either, but when I bite into that first big, juicy tomato, snap a crisp green bean or slice a tangy clove of fresh garlic, it's worth the work! Though by now most of the plants are probably shriveled and dead—if I'm lucky I may still have a sprig or two of broccoli to pick—that's okay. I get to start it all over again in a few months!

Best,

Michelle

MICHELLE CELMER

CAROSELLI'S CHRISTMAS BABY

HARLEQUIN®

entertain, enrich, inspire™

Recycling programs
for this product may
not exist in your area.

ISBN-13: 978-0-373-73207-4

CAROSELLI'S CHRISTMAS BABY

Copyright © 2012 by Michelle Celmer

This edition published by arrangement with Harlequin Books S.A.

For questions and comments about the quality of this book, please contact us at CustomerService@Harlequin.com.

® and TM are trademarks of Harlequin Enterprises Limited or its corporate affiliates. Trademarks indicated with ® are registered in the United States Patent and Trademark Office, the Canadian Trade Marks Office and in other countries.

www.Harlequin.com

Printed in U.S.A.

MICHELLE CELMER

is a bestselling author of more than thirty books. When she's not writing, she likes to spend time with her husband, kids, grandchildren and a menagerie of animals.

Michelle loves to hear from readers. Visit her website, www.michellecelmer.com, like her on Facebook, or write her at P.O. Box 300, Clawson, MI 48017.

For Steve, who truly is my hero.

Prologue

"As your attorney, and your friend, I have to say, Giuseppe, that I think this is a really bad idea."

Giuseppe Caroselli sat in his wingback leather chair—the one his wife, Angelica, God rest her saintly soul, had surprised him with for his eighty-fifth birthday—while Marcus Russo eyed him furtively from the sofa. And he was was right. This scheme Giuseppe had concocted had the potential to blow up in his face, and create another rift in a family that already had its share of quarrels. But he was an old man and time was running low. He could sit back and do nothing, but the potential outcome was too heartbreaking to imagine. He had to do *something*.

"It must be done," he told Marcus. "I've waited long enough."

"I can't decide which would be worse," Marcus said, rising from the sofa and walking to the window that boasted a picturesque view of the park across the street, though most of the leaves had already fallen. "If they say no, or they actually say yes."

"They've left me no choice. For the good of the family, it must be done." Carrying on the Caroselli legacy had always been his number one priority. It was the reason he had fled Italy at the height of the Second World War, speaking not a word of English, with a only few dollars in the pocket of his trousers and his *nonni's* secret family chocolate recipe emblazoned in his memory. He knew the Caroselli name was destined for great things.

He'd worked scrimped and saved until he had the money to start the first Caroselli Chocolate shop in downtown Chicago. In the next sixty years the Caroselli name grew to be recognized throughout the world, yet now it was in danger of dying out forever. Of his eight grandchildren and six great-grandchildren, there wasn't a single heir to carry on the family name. Though his three sons each had a son, they were all still single and seemed to have no desire whatsoever to marry and start families of their own.

Giuseppe had no choice but to take matters into his own hands, and make them an offer they simply could not refuse.

There was a soft rap on the study door, and the butler appeared, tall and wiry and nearly as old as his charge. "They're here, sir."

Right on time, Giuseppe thought with a smile. If there was one thing that could be said about his grandsons, they were unfailingly reliable. They were also as ambitious as Giuseppe had been at their age, which is why he believed this might work. "Thank you, William. Send them in."

The butler nodded and slipped from the room. A few seconds later his grandsons filed in. First Nicolas, charming and affable, with a smile that had been known to get him out of trouble with authority, and into trouble with the ladies. Following him was Nick's cousin Robert, serious, focused and unflinchingly loyal. And last but not least, the oldest of all his grandchildren, ambitious, dependable Antonio Junior.

His joints protesting the movement, Giuseppe rose from his chair. "Thank you for coming, boys." He gestured to the couch. "Please, have a seat."

They did as he asked, all three looking apprehensive.

"You are obviously curious as to why you're here," Giuseppe said, easing back into his chair.

"I'd like to know why we had to keep it a secret," Nick said, his brow furrowed with worry. "And why is Marcus here? Is something wrong?"

"Are you ill?" Tony asked.

"Fit as a fiddle," Giuseppe said. Or as fit as an arthritic man of ninety-two could be. "There is a matter of great importance we must discuss."

"Is the business in trouble?" Rob asked. For him, the company always came first, which was both a blessing and a curse. Had he not been so career-focused, he could be married with children by now. They all could.

"This isn't about the business," he told them. "At least, not directly. This is about the Caroselli family name, which will die unless the three of you marry and have sons."

That earned him a collective eye roll from all three boys.

"*Nonno,* we've been through this before," Nick said. "I for one am not ready to settle down. And I think I speak for all of us when I say that another lecture isn't going to change that."

"I know, that's why this time I've decided to offer an incentive."

That got their attention. Tony leaned forward slightly and asked, "What sort of incentive?"

"In a trust I have placed the sum of thirty million dollars to be split three ways when each of you marries and produces a male heir."

Three jaws dropped in unison.

Nick was the first to recover. "You're seriously going to give us each ten *million* dollars to get hitched and have a kid?"

"A *son*. And there are conditions."

"If you're going to try to force us into arranged marriages with nice Italian girls from the homeland, forget it," Rob said.

If only he could be so lucky. And while he would love to see each of them marry a nice Italian girl, he was in no position to be picky. "You're free to marry whomever you please."

"So what's the catch?" Tony asked.

"First, you cannot tell a soul about the arrangement. Not your parents or your siblings, not even your intended. If you do, you forfeit your third of the trust and it will be split between the other two."

"And?" Nick said.

"If I should join your *nonni,* God rest her saintly soul, by the end of the second year and before a male heir is born to any one of you, the trust will be rolled back into my estate."

"So the clock is ticking," Nick said.

"Maybe. Of course, I could live to be one hundred. My doctor tells me that I'm in excellent health. But is that a chance any of you is willing to take? If you agree to my terms, that is."

"What about Jessica?" Nick asked. "She has four children, yet I suspect you've not given her a dime."

"I love your sister, Nick, and all my granddaughters, but their children will never carry the Caroselli name. I owe it to my parents, and my grandparents, and those who lived before them to keep the family name alive for future generations. But I also don't want to see my granddaughters hurt, which is why this must always remain a secret."

"Do you intend to have us sign some sort of contract?" Tony asked, turning to Marcus.

"That was my suggestion," Marcus told him, "but your grandfather refuses."

"No one will be signing anything," Giuseppe said. "You'll just have to trust that my word is good."

"Of course we trust your word, *Nonno*," Nick said, shooting the others a look. "You've never given us any reason not to."

"I feel the same way about the three of you. Which is why I trust you to keep our arrangement private."

Tony frowned. "What if you die? Won't the family learn about it then?"

"They won't suspect a thing. The money is already put aside, separate from the rest of my fortune, and as my attorney and executor to my will, Marcus and Marcus alone will have access to it. He will see that the money is distributed accordingly."

"What if we aren't ready to start families?" Rob asked.

Giuseppe shrugged. "Then you lose out on ten million dollars, and your third will go to your cousins."

All three boys glanced at each other. Knowing how proud and independent they were, there was still the very real possibility that they might deny his request.

"Do you expect an answer today?" Nick asked.

"No, but I would at least like your word that each of you will give my offer serious thought."

Another look was exchanged, then all three nodded.

"Of course we will, *Nonno*," Rob said.

Had he been standing, Giuseppe may have crumpled with relief, and if not for gravity holding him to the earth, the heavy weight lifted from his stooped shoulders surely would have set him aloft. It wasn't a guarantee, but they hadn't outright rejected the idea, either, and that was a start. And given their competitive natures, he was quite positive that if one agreed, the other two would eventually follow suit.

After several minutes of talk about the business and family, Nick, Rob and Tony left.

"So," Marcus asked, as the study door snapped closed behind them, "how do you suppose they'll react when they learn there is no thirty million dollars set aside?"

Giuseppe shrugged. "I think they will be so blissfully happy, and so grateful for my timely intervention, that the money will mean nothing to them."

"You have the money, Giuseppe. Have you considered actually giving it to them if they meet your terms?"

"And alienate my other grandchildren?" he scoffed. "What sort of man do you think I am?"

Marcus shook his head with exasperation. "And if you're wrong? If they do want the money? If they're angry that you lied to them?"

"They won't be." Besides, to carry on the Caroselli name—his legacy—that was a risk he was willing to take.

One

Late again.

Terri Phillips watched with a mix of irritation and amusement as her best friend, Nick Caroselli, walked briskly through the dining room of the bistro to their favorite booth near the bar, where they met every Thursday night for dinner.

With his jet-black hair, smoldering brown eyes, warm olive complexion and lean physique, heads swiveled and forks halted halfway to mouths as he passed. But Nick being Nick, he didn't seem to notice. Not that he was unaware of his effect on women, nor was he innocent of using his charm to get his way when the need arose.

Not that it worked on her anymore.

"Sorry I'm late," he said with that crooked grin he flashed when he was trying to get out of trouble. Fat snowflakes peppered the shoulders of his wool coat and dotted his hair, and his cheeks were rosy from the cold, meaning he'd walked the two blocks from the world headquarters of Caroselli Chocolate. "Work was crazy today."

"I've only been here a few minutes," she said, even though it had actually been more like twenty. Long enough to have downed two glasses of the champagne they were supposed to be toasting with.

He leaned in to brush a kiss across her cheek, the rasp of his evening stubble rough against her skin. She breathed in the whisper of his sandalwood soap—a birthday gift from her—combined with the sweet scent of chocolate that clung to him every time he spent the day in the company test kitchen.

"Still snowing?" she asked.

"It's practically a blizzard out there." Nick shrugged out of his coat, then stuck his scarf and leather gloves in the sleeve—a habit he'd developed when they were kids, after misplacing endless sets of mittens and scarves—then hung it on the hook behind their booth. "At this rate, we may actually get a white Christmas this year."

"That would be nice." Having spent the first nine years of her life in New Mexico, she'd never even seen snow until she'd moved to Chicago. To this day, she still loved it. Of course, having a home business meant no snowy commute, so she was biased.

"I ordered our usual," she said as Nick slid into his seat.

He loosened his tie, and gestured to the champagne bottle. "Are we celebrating something?"

"You could say that."

He plucked his napkin from the table and draped it across his lap. "What's up?"

"First," she said, "you'll be happy to know that I broke up with Blake."

Nick beamed. "Well, damn, that is a reason to celebrate!"

Nick had never liked her most recent boyfriend—the latest in a long and depressing string of failed relationships. He didn't think Blake had what it took to make Terri happy. Turned out he was right. Even if it did take her four months to see it.

But last week Blake had mentioned offhandedly that his lease was almost up, and it seemed silly that they should both be paying rent when he spent most of his time at her place, anyway. Despite being more than ready to get married and start a family, when she imagined doing it with him, she'd felt...well, not much of anything, actually. Which was definitely not a good way to feel about a potential husband and father of her children. It was proof that, as Nick had warned her, she was settling again.

Nick poured himself a glass of champagne and took a sip. "So, what did he say when you dumped him?"

"That I'll never find anyone else like him."

Nick laughed. "Well, yeah, isn't that the point? He was about as interesting as a paper clip. With half the personality."

She wouldn't deny that he'd been a little, well...bland. His idea of a good time was sitting at the computer, with it's twenty-seven-inch high-def monitor, for hours on end playing *World of Warcraft* while she watched television or read. The truth is, he would probably miss her computer more than her.

"He's an okay guy. He just isn't the guy for me," she told Nick. One day he would meet the game addict of his dreams and they would live a long happy life in cyberspace together.

Their waitress appeared to deliver their meal. A double pepperoni deep-dish pizza and cheesy bread. When she was gone, Nick said, "He's out there, you know. The one for you. You'll find him."

She used to think so, too. But here she was almost thirty with not a single prospect anywhere in her near future. Her life plan had her married with a couple kids already. Which is why she had decided to take matters into her own hands.

"There's something else we're celebrating," she told Nick. "I'm going to have a baby."

He bolted upright and set down his glass so hard she was surprised it didn't shatter against the tiled tabletop. "What? When? Is it Blake's?"

"God, no!" She could just imagine that. The kid would probably be born with a game remote fused to its hands.

Nick leaned forward and hissed under his breath, "Whoever it is, he damn well better be planning to do right by you and the baby."

Always looking out for her, she thought with a shot of affection so intense it burned. When he wasn't getting her into trouble, that is. Although it was usually the other way around. It was typically her making rash decisions, and Nick talking sense into her. This time was different. This time she knew exactly what she was doing.

"There is no *who*," she told him, dishing them each out a slice of pizza. "I'm not actually pregnant. Yet."

Nick frowned. "Then why did you say you're having a baby?"

"Because I will be, hopefully within the next year. I'm going to be a single mom."

He sat back in his seat, looking stunned. "How? I mean, who's going to be the father?"

"I'm going to use a donor."

"A *donor?*" His dark brows pulled together. "You're not serious."

She shoved down the deep sting of disappointment. She had hoped he would understand, that he would be happy for her. Clearly, he wasn't. "Completely serious. I'm ready. I'm financially sound, and since I work at home, I won't have to put the baby in day care. The timing is perfect."

"Wouldn't it be better if you were married?"

"I've pretty much struck out finding Mr. Right. I always said that I wanted to have my first baby by the time I'm thirty, and I'm almost there. And you know that I've always wanted a family of my own. Since my aunt died, I've got no one."

"You've got me," he said, his expression so earnest her heart melted.

Yes, she had him, not to mention his entire crazy family, but it wasn't the same. When the chips were down, she was still an outsider.

"This doesn't mean we aren't going to be friends still," she said. "In fact, I'll probably need you more than ever. You'll be the baby's only other family. Uncle Nicky."

The sentiment did nothing to erase the disenchantment from his expression. He pushed away his plate, as if he'd suddenly lost his appetite, and said, "You deserve better than a sperm donor."

"I don't exactly have the best luck with men."

"But what about the baby?" Nick said, sounding testier by the second. "Doesn't it deserve to have two parents?"

"As you well know, having two parents doesn't necessarily make for a happy childhood."

His deepening frown said that he knew she was right. Though he didn't like to admit it, his childhood had left deep, indelible scars.

"I was hoping you would understand," she said, and for some stupid reason she felt like crying. And she hardly *ever* cried. At least, not in front of other people. All it had ever earned her from her aunt—who didn't have a sympathetic bone in her body—was a firm lecture.

"I do," Nick said, reaching across the table for her hand. "I just want you to be happy."

"This *will* make me happy."

He smiled and gave her hand a squeeze. "Then I'm happy, too."

She hoped he really meant that. That he wasn't just humoring her. But as they ate their pizza and chatted, Nick seemed distracted, and she began to wonder if telling him about having a baby had been a bad idea, although for the life of her she wasn't sure why it would matter either way to him.

After they finished eating, they put on their coats and were walking to the door when Nick asked, "Did you drive or take the bus?"

"Bus," she said. If she thought she might be drinking, she always opted for public transportation. If the man who had plowed into her father's car had only been as responsible, she wouldn't be an orphan.

"Walk back to the office with me and I'll drive you home."

"Okay."

The snow had stopped, but a prematurely cold wind whipped her hair around her face and the pavement was slippery, which made the two-block hike tricky. It was how she rationalized the fact that he was unusually quiet and there was a deep furrow in his brow.

When they got to the Caroselli Chocolate world headquarters building, it was closed for the night, so Nick used a key card to let them in. With a retail store taking up most of the ground floor, the lobby smelled of the chocolate confections lining the shelves. Everything from standard chocolate bars to gourmet chocolate-covered apples.

Nick felt around in his pockets, then cursed under his breath. "I left my car keys in my office."

"You want me to wait down here?"

"No, you can come up." Then he grinned and said, "Unless you're an industrial spy trying to steal the Caroselli secret recipe."

"Right, because we both know what an accomplished cook I am." If there were a way to burn water, she would figure it out. Meaning she ordered out a lot, and the rest of the time ate microwave dinners.

They walked past the receptionist's desk and he used his key card to activate the elevator. Only authorized personnel and approved visitors were allowed above the ground floor. And no one but the Caroselli family and employees with special clearance were allowed in the test kitchen.

Nick was quiet the entire ride up to the fourth floor, and while they walked down the hall to his office. She had to smile as he opened the door and switched on the light, and she saw the lopsided stacks of papers and memos on the surface of his desk, leaving no space at all to work. She suspected that this was why he spent so much time on the top floor in the kitchen.

He opened the desk drawer and pulled out his car keys, but then he just stood there. Something was definitely bugging him and she needed to know what.

"What's the matter, Nick? And don't tell me nothing. I've known you long enough to know when something is wrong."

"I've just been thinking."

"About me having a baby?"

He nodded.

"It's what I want."

"Then there's something we need to talk about."

"Okay," she said, her heart sinking just the tiniest bit, mostly because he wouldn't look at her. And he must have been anticipating a long discussion because he took off his coat and tossed it over the back of his chair. She did the same, then nudged aside a pile of papers so she could sit beside him on the edge of his desk.

He was quiet for several long seconds, as though he was working something through in his head, then he looked at her and said, "You really want to do it? Have a baby, I mean."

"I really do."

"What if I had a better way?"

"A better way?"

He nodded. "For both of us."

Both of them? She failed to see how her plan to have a baby could in any way benefit him. "I'm not sure what you mean."

"I know the perfect man to be the father of your baby. Someone who would actually be around. Someone willing to take financial responsibility for the rest of the baby's life."

Whoever this so-called perfect man was, he sounded too good to be true. "Oh, yeah?" she said. "Who?"

He leaned forward, his dark eyes serious. "Me."

For a second she was too stunned to speak. Nick wanted to have a baby with her? "Why? You've been pretty adamant about the fact that you don't want children."

"Trust me when I say that it will be a mutually advantageous arrangement."

"Advantageous how?"

"What I'm about to tell you, you have to promise not to repeat to anyone. *Ever.*"

"Okay."

"Say, 'I promise.'"

She rolled her eyes. What were they, twelve? *"I promise."*

"Last week my grandfather called me, Rob and Tony to his house for a secret meeting. He offered us ten million dollars each to produce a male heir to carry on the Caroselli name."

"Holy crap."

"That was pretty much my first reaction, too. I wasn't sure I was even going to accept his offer. I'm really not ready to settle down, but then you mentioned your plan…" He shrugged. "I mean, how much more perfect could it be? You get the baby you want and I get the money."

It made sense in a weird way, but her and *Nick?*

"Of course, we would have to get married," he said.

Whoa, wait a minute. *"Married?* Haven't you told me about a million times that you'll *never* get married?"

"You know how traditional *Nonno* is. I don't have a choice. But the minute I have the cash in hand, we can file for a quickie divorce. An ironclad prenup should eliminate any complications…not that I expect there would be any."

"That sounds almost too easy."

"Well, we will have to make it look convincing."

Why did she get the feeling she wasn't going to like this? "What exactly do you mean by *convincing?*"

"You'll have to move into my place."

A fake marriage was one thing, but to *live* together? "I don't think that's a good idea."

"I have lots of space. You can have the spare bedroom and you can turn the den into your office."

Space wasn't the issue. They'd tried the roommate thing right after college, in an apartment more than spacious enough for two people. Between the random girls parading in and out at ridiculous hours—and the fact that Nick never picked up after himself and left the sink filled with his dirty dishes while the dishwasher sat empty, and a couple dozen other annoying quirks and habits he had—after two months she'd reached her limit. Had she stayed even a day longer, it would have either killed their friendship, or she would have killed him.

"Nick, you know I love you, and I value our friendship beyond anything else, but we've tried this before. It didn't work."

"That was almost eight years ago. I'm sure we've both matured since then."

"Have you stopped being a slob, too? Because I loathe the thought of spending the next nine months cleaning up after you."

"You won't have to. I have a cleaning service come in three times a week. And for the record, I'm not particularly looking forward to you nagging me incessantly."

"I do not nag," she said, and he shot her a look. "Okay, maybe I nag a little, but only out of sheer frustration."

"Then we'll just have to make an effort to be more accommodating to each other. I promise to keep on top of the clutter, if you promise not to nag."

That might be easier said than done.

"Think how lucky the kid will be," Nick said. "Most divorced parents hate each other. Mine haven't had a civilized conversation in years. His will be best friends."

He had a good point there. "So that means you'll be a regular part of the baby's life?"

"Of course. And he'll have lots of cousins, and aunts and uncles."

Wasn't a part-time father better than no father at all? And she would never have to worry financially. She knew Nick would take care of the baby. Not that she was hurting for money. If she was careful, the trust her aunt had willed her, combined with her growing web design business, would keep her living comfortably for a very long time. But Nick would see that the baby went to the best schools, and had every advantage, things she couldn't quite afford. And he would be a part of a big, loving, happy family. Which was more than she could say for her own childhood. The baby might even join the Caroselli family business some day.

"And suppose, God forbid, something should happen to you," he said. "Where would the baby go if he was fathered by a donor?"

Having lost her own parents, of course that was a concern. Now that her aunt was gone, there was no family left to take the child if she were in an accident or... Although the baby would probably be better off in foster care than with someone like her aunt. She would have been.

"With me as the father, he'll always have a family." Nick said.

As completely crazy as the idea was, it did make sense. "I think it could work."

He actually looked excited, although who wouldn't be over the prospect of ten million bucks? Why settle for the life of a millionaire when he could be a *multi*millionaire?

"So," he said, "is that an 'I'm still thinking about it,' or is that a definite yes?"

Though she was often guilty for jumping into things without full consideration, maybe in this case overthinking it would be a bad idea. Or maybe she just didn't want the opportunity to talk herself out of it. They would both be getting what they wanted. More or less.

"I just have one more question," she said. "What about women?"

"What about them?"

"Will it be a different girl every other night? Will I have to listen to the moaning and the headboard knocking against the wall? See her traipsing around the next morning in nothing but her underwear and one of your shirts?"

"Of course not. As long as we're married, I wouldn't see anyone else."

"Nick, we're talking at least nine months. Can you even go that long without dating?"

"Do you really mean *dating,* or is that code for sex?"

"Either."

"Can you?"

She could. The real question was, did she want to? But to have a baby, wasn't it worth it?

"Maybe," Nick said, "we don't have to."

"Are you suggesting that we cheat on each other?" Even if it wasn't a real marriage, that could be an obstacle. And while she was sure Nick would have no trouble finding willing participants, with her big belly and swelling ankles, she was fairly certain no men would be fighting for the chance to get into her maternity jeans.

"I'm assuming you plan to use artificial insemination," he said.

She felt a little weird about discussing the particulars, but he was a part of this now. It would be his baby, too. "That or in vitro, which is much more reliable, but crazy expensive. Either way it could take several months."

"Or we could pay nothing at all," he said.

She must have looked thoroughly confused, because he laughed and said, "You have no idea what I'm talking about."

"I guess I don't."

"Think about it." He wiggled his eyebrows and flashed her a suggestive smile.

Wait a minute. He couldn't possibly mean—

"Why pay a doctor to get you pregnant," he said, "when we could just do it the old-fashioned way for free?"

Two

Terri gaped at Nick, her eyes—which were sometimes green and sometimes blue, depending on the light—wide with shock and horror. It took her several seconds to find her voice, and when she did, she said, a full octave higher than her usual range, "That was a joke, right?"

"Actually, I've never been more serious." Nick would be the first to admit it was a pretty radical idea, but on a scale of one to ten, this entire situation had a weird factor of about fifty.

He had given *Nonno's* offer a lot of thought and had come to the conclusion that he just wasn't ready to settle down yet. It wasn't so much the idea of being a father that put him off—he loved kids—but the marriage end of the deal that gave him the willies. His parents had gone through hell, and put Nick and his two older sisters through it, too. Now with his sister Jessica's marriage in trouble, as well, the idea of marital bliss was nothing more than a fairy tale to him. And not worth the pain of the inevitable divorce. Not even for ten million dollars.

It had never occurred to him that the actual marriage could be a sham. Not to mention so mutually advantageous. And who in his family would question the plausibility that after twenty years of devoted friendship, his and Terri's relationship had moved to the next level? The women in his family ate up that kind of romantic garbage.

Terri tucked her long dark hair behind her ears. He'd only seen her do this when she was nervous or uncomfortable, and that wasn't very often. She was one of the most centered, secure and confident people he'd ever known. Sometimes this led to her being a touch impulsive, but in this instance could only work in his favor.

"The sooner this kid is born, the better," he told her. "So why would we spend a lot of time and money on procedures that could take months to work?"

Indecision wrinkled the space between her brows and she picked at the frayed cuff of her sweatshirt. "Aren't you worried that it might make things weird between us?" she asked.

"Maybe a little," he admitted. "But, haven't you ever been curious?"

"Curious?"

He gave her arm a gentle nudge. "You've never wondered what it might be like if you and I…"

It took an awful lot to embarrass her, but there was a distinct red hue working its way across her cheekbones. That was a yes if he'd ever seen one, even if she didn't want to admit it. And he couldn't deny that he'd thought about it himself more than a time or two. She was funny and smart and beautiful, so who could blame him?

"I've never told you this," he said. "But there was a time when I had a pretty serious crush on you."

She blinked. "You did?"

He nodded. "Yep."

"When?"

"Our junior year of high school."

She looked genuinely stunned. "I—I had no idea."

That's because he'd never said a word about it. Up until then, he'd never viewed her in a sexual way. Nor, it seemed, did many other boys. She had been a late bloomer, a typical tomboy, lanky and tall—taller than all the other girls and even a fair share of the boys—and as far from feminine as a girl could be. But she'd spent the entire summer after their sophomore year in Europe with her aunt and something intriguing had happened. She left Chicago a girl, and returned a woman.

Boys in school began paying attention to her, talking about her in the locker room, and he wouldn't deny that she became the subject of a few of his own teenage fantasies. Not that he would have acted on those feelings. They were, after all, only friends, though that fact did little to erase the jealousy he felt when he saw her with other boys, or would hear the rumors of the things she had done with them. And as much as he liked how she changed, he resented her for it. He wanted the old Terri back. But he got over it, of course. What choice did he have?

"Why didn't you tell me?" she asked.

"Aside from the fact that I thought it would probably freak you out?" He shrugged. "It was a crush. I had them all the time. And our friendship was too important to me to ruin over raging teenage hormones."

"But you would be willing to ruin it now?"

"Maybe if we were sleeping together just for the sake of doing it, but this is different. We have a legitimate reason to have sex."

In his experience, romantic love and friendship occupied opposite sides of the playing field, and he would never let one interfere with the other. Which is why he was so sure that if they approached this situation logically, it would work. And when all was said and done, everyone would get exactly what they wanted.

"It's a means to an end," he said. "It wouldn't *mean anything*."

She shot him a look. "That's just what every girl wants to hear when she's considering sleeping with a man."

"You get my point. And yes, it could potentially change our relationship, but not necessarily for the worse. It might even bring us closer together."

She didn't look convinced. Maybe she was opposed to the idea for an entirely different reason.

"Do you have moral objections?" he asked. "Or is it just that you find the idea of sleeping with me revolting?"

She rolled her eyes. "You are *not* revolting. And though it's embarrassing to admit, I had kind of a crush on you once, too."

If that was true, she'd done one hell of a job hiding it. "When?"

"It pretty much started the day I transferred into Thomas Academy school in fourth grade."

He recalled that day clearly, when she'd walked into his class, bitter, sullen and mad as hell. It was obvious to everyone in the elite private school that she was an outsider. And trouble. A fact she drove home that very first day when she had come up behind Nick on the playground and pushed him off his swing, knocking him face-first in the dirt. He wanted to shove her right back, but he'd had it drilled into him by his mother to respect girls, so he'd walked away instead. Which only seemed to fuel her lust for blood.

For days he'd tolerated kicks in the shin, pinches on

the arm, prods in the cafeteria line and endless ribbing from his buddies for not retaliating. With his parents in the middle of a nasty divorce, he'd had some anger issues of his own, and the unprovoked attacks started to grate on him. A week or so later she tripped him on his way to the lunch table, making him drop his tray and spill his spaghetti and creamed corn all over the cafeteria floor and himself. The other students laughed, and something inside Nick snapped. Before he realized what he was doing, he hauled off and popped her one right in the mouth.

The entire cafeteria went dead silent, everyone watching to see what would happen next, and he'd felt instantly ashamed for hitting a weak, defenseless girl.

He would never forget the way he'd stood watching her, waiting for the tears to start as blood oozed from the corner of her lip and down her chin. And how she balled her fist, took a swing right back at him, clipping him in the jaw. He was so stunned, he just stood there. But she wasn't finished. She launched herself at him, knocking him to the floor, and there was nothing girly about it. No biting or scratching or hair-pulling. She fought like a boy, and her fists were lethal weapons. He had no choice but to fight back. To defend himself. Plus, he had his pride, because to a nine-year-old boy, being accepted meant everything.

It had taken three teachers to pry them apart and haul them to the dean's office, both of them bruised and bloody. They were given a fourteen-day in-school suspension, though that was mild compared to the tirade he'd endured from his father, and the disappointment from his mother, who he knew were miserable enough without any help from him.

He spent the next two weeks holed up in a classroom alone with Terri, and as the black eyes faded and the split lips healed, something weird happened. To this day he wasn't sure whether it was mutual admiration or two lost souls finding solace in each other, but they walked out of that room friends, and had been ever since.

"So, you beat the snot out of me because you *liked* me?" he said.

"It wasn't even a conscious thing. Until I looked back at it years later did I realize why I was so mean to you. But once we became friends, I never thought about you in a romantic way."

"Never?"

"Why would I?" she said, but a hot-pink blush crept up into her cheeks. She pushed herself off his desk and walked over to the window, looking out into the darkness, at the traffic crawling past on icy roads.

If she hadn't, why the embarrassment? Why was she running away from him?

He knew he should probably let it go, but he couldn't. "You never thought about what it might be like if I kissed you?"

With her back to him, she shrugged. "You kiss me all the time."

"Not a real kiss." But now that he'd gotten the idea into his head, he couldn't seem to shake it off. He *wanted* to kiss her.

He pushed off the desk, walked over to the window and stood behind her. He put his hands on her shoulders and she jerked, sucking in a surprised breath. "Nick…"

He turned her so she was facing him. She was so tall they were practically nose to nose. "Come on, aren't you the least bit curious?"

"It's just…it would be weird."

He propped a hand on the windowpane beside her

head, so she was blocked in by his arm on one side and the wall on the other. "How will you know until you try?"

He reached up to run his finger down her cheek, and not only was it crimson, but burning hot.

"Nick," she said, but it came out sounding low and breathy. It was a side of her that he didn't see often. A softer, vulnerable Terri, and he liked it. And it occurred to him, as he leaned in closer, that what he was feeling right now wasn't just curiosity. He was turned-on. And it was no longer the childish fantasies of a teenage boy who knew he wanted something, but wasn't quite sure what it was. This time Nick knew exactly what he wanted.

"One kiss," he told her, coming closer, so his mouth was just inches from hers. "And if it's really that awful, we won't ever do it again."

Heat rolled off her in waves. Her pulse was racing, and as she tentatively laid a hand near the collar of his jacket, he could feel her trembling. Was she afraid, or as sexually charged by this as he was? Or was it a little of both? With her hand strategically placed on his chest, she could either push him away, or grab his lapel and pull him in.

Which would it be?

He leaned in slowly, drawing out the suspense. When his lips were a fraction of an inch away, so near he could feel the flutter of her breath, as her fingers curled around the lapel of his jacket…a loud noise from the hallway startled them both and they jumped apart.

Damn it!

Nick walked to the door and looked out to see a member of the cleaning crew pushing her cart down the hall toward the conference room.

He turned, hoping they could pick up where they left off, only to find Terri yanking on her coat. "What are you doing?"

"I really need to get home."

"Terri—"

"This was a mistake, Nick. I think we're better off using a doctor, like I originally planned."

"If that's what you really want," he said, feeling disappointed, but trying not to let it show.

"I'll cover the cost."

As if he would let her do that. "I insist on paying at least half."

She looked as if she might argue, then seemed to change her mind. She nodded and said, "That sounds fair."

He grabbed his coat and shrugged into it. "I'll drive you home."

She didn't say a word as they walked to the elevator, and rode it to the underground parking garage, but he could practically hear the wheels in her mind moving. As much as he wanted to know what she was thinking, he knew better than to ask. If she wanted him to know, she would talk when she was ready. If he tried to drag it out of her, she would clam up. He'd seen her do it a million times. As close as they were, there was always a small part of herself that she vigilantly guarded from everyone, and could he blame her? His parents' relationship may have been a disaster, but at least he had parents. Despite their dysfunctional marriage, they loved him and his sisters. From the time she moved to Chicago, all Terri ever had was an aunt who only tolerated her presence. If she had loved Terri, she had been unable, or unwilling to let it show.

Though he knew it irked her, Nick opened the passenger door for Terri. Normally she would make a fuss about being completely capable of opening her own door thank-you-very-much, but she didn't say a word this time. Anyone who knew Terri was well aware she always had something to say, or an opinion about pretty much everything. Tonight, she was quiet the entire ride to her condominium complex on the opposite side of town.

Nick pulled up in front of her unit and turned to her, but she was just sitting there, looking out the windshield. "Everything okay?" he asked.

She nodded, but didn't move.

"Are you sure? You can talk to me."

"I know. I just…" She shrugged.

Whatever it was, she wasn't ready to discuss it.

"Well, you know where I am if you need me," he said, even though as long as he'd known her, Terri never truly *needed* anyone. She wrote the handbook on self-sufficiency.

He leaned over to kiss her cheek, the way he always did, but she flung open the car door and jumped out before he had the chance. As he watched her dart into the building without looking back, he couldn't help thinking that in her attempt to keep things between them from changing, they already had.

Three

Though she had hoped getting a good night's sleep would make things clearer, Terri tossed and turned all night, then woke the next morning feeling just as confused as she had been when Nick had dropped her at home.

She didn't want their relationship to change. But what she realized last night while he drove her home was that it already had changed, and it was too late to go back. They had opened a door, and there would be no closing it again until they both stepped through. Unfortunately, she had no idea what was waiting on the other side.

After a long and unproductive workday spent wondering what to do next, how they could pull this off without killing their friendship—if they hadn't already—she realized that she'd made her decision last night in his office. She'd just been too afraid to admit it. Not only to him, but to herself. Which was what led her to his apartment this evening. He hadn't tried to contact her all day, by phone or even email, meaning that he was smart enough to realize she needed time to work this through on her own. He was always there when she needed him, but he also knew when she needed space. She realized it said an awful lot about their relationship.

He opened the door dressed in jeans and a T-shirt, with a chef's apron tied around his waist and smudged with what looked like chocolate batter. The scent of something sweet and delicious reached out into the hallway to greet her.

"Hey," he said, looking not at all surprised to see her.

"Can we talk?"

"Of course." He stepped aside to let her in, and she gazed around the high-rise apartment that would be home for the next nine months or so. It was painted in rich, masculine hues, yet it still managed to feel warm and homey, in large part due to the casual-comfy furnishings and the dozens of framed family photos throughout the space.

Nick may have had an aversion to marriage, but when it came to his family, he couldn't be more devoted. She was also happy to see that most of the clutter that had been there last week was gone.

"Come on into the kitchen," he said. "I'm trying a new cake recipe."

A culinary genius, he spent much of his free time cooking and baking. He'd often said that if it wasn't for Caroselli Chocolate, he would have opened his own restaurant, but he would never leave the family business.

On her way through the living room, Terri dropped her purse and coat on the sofa, then followed Nick into his state-of-the-art kitchen, half of which she wouldn't have the first clue how to use. Nor did she have the desire to learn.

"Whatever it is, it smells delicious," she told Nick as she took a seat on one of the three bar stools at the island.

"Triple chocolate fudge," he said. "Jess wants me to make something special for Angie's birthday party next Saturday."

"She'll be eleven, right?"

"Twelve."

"*Really?* Wow. I remember when she was born, how excited you were to be an uncle. It doesn't seem like twelve years ago."

"It goes by fast," he said, checking the contents of one of the three top-of-the-line wall ovens. Then he untied the apron and draped it over the oven door handle—where it would probably remain until someone else put it in the broom closet where it belonged. He leaned against the edge of the granite countertop, folded his arms and asked, "So, enough of the small talk. What's up?"

That was Nick, always getting right to the point. "First, I want to apologize for the way I acted last night. You just…surprised me."

"It's okay. You were a little overwhelmed. I get it."

"But I've been giving it a lot of thought. In fact, it's about the only thing I *can* think about, and I just have one more question."

"Shoot."

"If we do this, if we make the baby the old-fashioned way, can you promise me that afterward things will go back to the way they were? That nothing will change?"

"No. I can't promise that."

She sighed. Did he have to be so damned honest? Couldn't he just humor her into thinking she was making the right choice? But that wasn't Nick. He was a straight shooter, and the only time he sugarcoated was in the kitchen.

"The best I can do is promise you that I'll always be there for you," he said. "We'll always be friends. Whether we use a doctor or do this conventionally, we're going to have a child together. That alone is bound to change things."

He was right, of course. She'd been so focused on the idea of how sleeping together would affect their relationship, that she hadn't truly grasped the enormity of having a child together. She'd wanted a baby so badly, she hadn't let herself fully consider the consequences. She realized now that *everything* would change. The question was, would it be a good change?

"I guess I didn't think this through completely," she told Nick. "Big surprise, right?"

"And now that you have?"

It scared her half to death. She'd been friends with Nick longer than anyone. Longer than she knew her own father. "I'm still hopelessly confused."

"Then we aren't going to do it. You can stick to your original plan and use a donor."

"And what will you do?" The idea of him entering a fake marriage with someone else, having a baby with her, left a knot in her belly.

"I won't do anything," he said.

"What do you mean?"

"I'll admit, I was sort of excited about the idea of having a baby, but only because I would be having it with you."

"But, what about the money?"

"Terri, our friendship means more to me than any sum of money."

She was too stunned to speak.

Nick laughed. "Why do you look so surprised?"

"It's just...I think that's probably the nicest thing anyone has ever said to me."

"I didn't say it to be nice. I said it because it's the truth."

And she felt ashamed that she hadn't trusted him, that she never realized just how much her friendship meant to him. "Let's do it," she said. "Let's have a baby."

Now he was the one who looked surprised. "Maybe you should take a little more time to consider this."

"I don't need more time."

"Are you sure?"

She couldn't recall ever feeling more sure about anything in her entire life. She didn't know why exactly. She just knew. "I want to do this."

"The wedding, the baby, moving in with me. Everything?"

"Everything."

"I guess the only question now is, how soon can we get started?" he asked.

"Well, I'm due to ovulate in two weeks, give or take a day or two. I'd rather not wait another month. The sooner I get pregnant, the better."

"The question is, can we plan a wedding in fourteen days?"

"I guess it depends on the kind of wedding you want."

"I would be happy to do this in front of a judge with a couple witnesses."

"That works for me," she said. Terri hadn't spent her adolescence dreaming of and planning her wedding. And why drop a lot of money on a marriage that was guaranteed to end in divorce?

"There's only one problem with that," he said.

She knew exactly what he was going to say. "Your family would have a fit." If there was one thing that the

Carosellis loved, it was a party. They would never pass up the opportunity to gather together, overeat and drink too much.

"Exactly," he said.

"So, how big are you thinking?"

"Immediate family only, maybe a few people from work."

"Two weeks would be the Saturday before Thanksgiving. I can guarantee most places will be booked."

Nick considered that for a moment, then his face lit up. "Hey, how about *Nonno*'s house? It would definitely be big enough. We could have the ceremony in the great room, in front of the fireplace."

"He wouldn't mind?"

"Are you kidding? He would be thrilled. The whole point of this is to get the three of us married off and making babies as soon as possible."

It seemed like a logical choice to her, too. "Call him and make sure it's okay. On such short notice, I'm thinking we should keep it as simple as possible. Drinks and appetizers will be the best way to go."

"My cousin Joe on my mom's side can get us a good deal on the liquor. Make a list of what you think we'll need, then remember that it's my family and whatever you plan to order, double it. And we should call the caterer we use for business events. The food is great, and their prices are reasonable."

"Email me the number and I'll call them." There was so much to do, and so little time. But she was sure they could pull it off. She knew that as soon as his mom and his sisters heard the news, they would be gunning to help.

"You understand that my family has to believe this marriage is real, that we have to look like two people madly in love?"

"I know."

"That means we'll have to appear comfortable kissing and touching each other."

The thought of kissing and touching Nick, especially in front of his family, made her heart skip a beat.

"Can you do that?" he asked.

Did she have a choice? "I can do it."

"Are you sure? Last night when I touched you, you jumped a mile."

"I was just nervous. And confused."

"And you aren't now?"

"I'm trying to look at it logically. Like we're just two people…conducting a science experiment."

Nick laughed. "That sounds fun. And correct me if I'm wrong, but didn't you almost blow up the science lab in middle school?"

Which had taught her the invaluable lesson that when a teacher said chemicals aren't to be mixed, she actually meant it. That, plus a week of suspension, and a month of summer school to make up the failing grade she'd more than earned in the class, drove the message home.

But what Nick seemed to be forgetting was she'd only done it because he'd *dared* her.

"I didn't think it was supposed to be fun," she said.

He frowned. "You don't think sex should be fun?"

"Not *all* sex. I guess I just thought, because we're friends, we would just sort of…go through the motions."

"There's no reason why we can't enjoy it," Nick said.

"What if we're not compatible?"

"As far as I'm aware, we both have the right parts," he said with a grin. "Unless there's something you haven't told me."

She rolled her eyes. "I don't mean *biologically* compatible. What if we get started and we don't get, you know... turned-on?"

"Are you saying you find me unattractive?"

"No, but in twenty years, I've never looked at you and had the uncontrollable urge to jump your bones. I just don't think of you that way."

"Come here," he said, summoning her around the island with a crooked finger.

"Why?"

"I'm going to kiss you."

Her heart skipped a beat. "Now?"

"Why not now? Before we go through the trouble of getting married, shouldn't we know for sure? Besides, what if we wait until our wedding day, and it all goes horribly wrong? Suppose we bump noses, or we both tilt our head the same way. And what about our honeymoon? Are we just going to hop into bed without ever having touched each other? Doesn't it make more sense for us to ease into it gradually?"

He definitely had a point. The problem here was that she was trying to play by a set of rules that didn't exist. They were making it up as they went along. "I guess that does make sense."

"So, what are you waiting for?" He tapped his lips with his index finger. "Lay one on me."

The idea that they were really going to do it, that he was going to kiss her for real, and not his usual peck on the cheek, gave her a funny feeling in her head. Her hands went all warm and tingly, as if all the blood in her body was pooling somewhere south of her heart.

It's just Nick. She had no reason to be nervous or scared or whatever it was she was feeling. But as her feet carried her around the island to where he stood, her heart was racing.

"Ready?" he asked, and she nodded.

Nick leaned in, but before their lips could meet, a giggle burst up from her chest. Nick drew back, looking exasperated.

"Sorry, I guess I'm a little nervous." She took a deep breath and blew it out, shaking the feeling back into her fingers. "I'm okay now. I promise not to laugh again."

"Good, because you're bruising my fragile ego."

Somehow she doubted that. She'd never met a man more secure in his prowess with women.

"Okay," he said. "Are you ready?"

"Ready."

"*Really* ready?"

She nodded. "Really ready."

Nick leaned in, and she met him halfway, and their lips just barely touched.

She couldn't help it, she giggled again.

Backing away, Nick sighed loudly. "This is not working."

"I am so sorry," she said. "I'm really trying."

Maybe this wasn't going to work. If she couldn't feel comfortable kissing him, what would it be like trying to have sex?

"Close your eyes," he said.

She narrowed them at him instead. "Why?"

"Just close them. And *keep* them closed."

Even though she felt stupid, she did as he asked, and for what felt like a full minute he did nothing, and she started to feel impatient. "Any day now."

"Shush."

Another thirty seconds or so passed and finally she felt him move closer, felt the whisper of his breath on her cheek, then his lips brushed over hers. This time she didn't giggle, and she wasn't so nervous anymore. His lips were soft and his evening stubble felt rough against her chin, but in a sexy way. And though it wasn't exactly passionate, it wasn't merely friendly, either.

This is nice, she thought. Nice enough that she wanted to see what came next, and when Nick started to pull away, before he could get too far, she fisted her hands in the front of his shirt and pulled him back in.

He made a sound, somewhere between surprise and pleasure, and he must have forgotten all about their ease-into-it-gradually plan, because it went from *nice* to *holy-cow-can-this-guy-kiss* in two seconds flat. He must have been sampling the cake batter earlier, because he tasted sweet, like chocolate.

Oh, my gosh, she was kissing *Nick,* her *best friend.* It was Nick's arms circling her, Nick's hand cupping her cheek, sliding under the root of her ponytail and cocking her head to just the right angle.

Her internal thermometer shot into the red zone and her bones began a slow melt, dripping away like icicles in the hot sun. And only when she heard Nick moan, when she felt her fingers sink through the softness of his hair, did she realize that her arms were around his shoulders, that her body was pressed against him, her breasts crushed against the hard wall of his chest. It was thrilling and arousing, and scary as hell, and a couple dozen other emotions all jumbled up together. But more than anything, it just felt…*right.* In a way that no other kiss had before. And all she could think was *more.*

For the second time Nick was the one to pull away, and she had to fight the urge to tighten her arms around his neck and pull him to her again. But instead of letting go completely, he hooked his fingers in the belt loop of her jeans.

"Wow," he said, searching her face, almost as if he were seeing her for the first time. "That was…"

"Wow," she agreed. If she had known kissing Nick would be like that, she might have tried it a long time ago.

"Are you still worried about us being incompatible?" he asked.

"Somehow I don't think that's going to be a problem."

"Do you feel weird?"

"Weird?"

"You said before that you were afraid things might get weird between us."

The only thing she felt right now was turned-on, and ready to kiss him again. "It's difficult to say after one kiss."

"Oh, really?" he said, tugging her closer. "Then I guess we'll just have to do it again."

Four

Their second kiss was even better than the first, and this time when Nick stopped and asked, "Feeling weird yet?" instead of answering, Terri just pulled him in for number three. And she was so wowed by the fact that it was Nick kissing her, Nick touching her, that she didn't really think about *where* he was touching her. Not until his hand slid down over the back pocket of her jeans, then everything came to a screeching halt.

She backed away and looked at him. "Your hand is on my butt."

"I know. I put it there." He paused, then said, "Am I moving too fast?"

Was he? Was it too much too soon? Was there some sort of schedule they were supposed to follow? A handbook for friends who become lovers to have a baby? As long as it felt good, as long as they both wanted it, why stop?

And boy, did it feel good.

"No," she said. "You're not moving too fast. If you were, would I be thinking how much better it would feel if my jeans were off?"

He made a growly noise deep in his chest and kissed her hard, but despite that shameless invitation into her pants, he kept his hands on the outside of her clothes. And no matter where she touched him, how she rubbed up against him, or encouraged him with little moans of pleasure, he didn't seem to be getting the hint that she was ready to proceed.

When he did finally slide his hand under her shirt, she felt like pumping her fist in the air, and shouting, "Yes!" But then he just kept it there. It wasn't that it didn't feel good resting just above the waist of her jeans, but she was sure it would feel a whole lot better eight inches or so higher and slightly to the left.

She pulled back and said, "If you felt the need to touch my breast, or pretty much any other part of my anatomy, I wouldn't stop you."

Looking amused, he said, "It's not often a woman tells me I'm moving too slow."

"I could play coy, but what's the point? We both know we're going to end up in bed tonight."

His brows rose. "We do?"

"Can you think of a reason we shouldn't?"

When most men would have jumped at the offer, he actually took several seconds to think about it. Which for some strange reason made her want it even more. It was crazy to think that on Wednesday she wouldn't have even considered a physical relationship with him, but two days and a couple kisses later, she couldn't wait to get him out of his clothes. And if he turned her down, she was going to be seriously unhappy.

After a brief pause he shrugged and said, "Nothing is coming to mind."

The way she figured it, their friendship had been leading up to this, even if they hadn't realized it. That equated to about twenty years of foreplay. Technically, no one could say they were rushing things. "So why are we still standing in the kitchen?"

He opened his mouth to answer her, when they heard the apartment door open. Terri's first thought was that it was another woman. Someone he was dating that he'd given a key to. Then she heard Nick's mom call, "Yoo-hoo! Nicky, I'm here!"

Nick muttered a curse. And here he thought the days of his mom interrupting while he was with a girl had ended when he moved away from home.

"In the kitchen," he called, then turned to Terri to apologize. But he never got the words out. Her hair was a mess, her clothes disheveled and she had beard burn all over her chin. Unless his mom had forgotten to put her contacts in that morning, it would be obvious that they'd been fooling around. He could hope that she wouldn't notice, but she noticed *everything,* and typically had an opinion she always felt compelled to share. Terri was a lot like her in that way.

Terri's eyes went wide, and she glanced at his crotch, but she didn't have to worry. He'd lost his erection the second he heard the door and remembered that his mom was stopping by.

"I can't believe this weather," his mom said, her voice growing louder as she walked toward the kitchen. "Two days ago we get a blizzard—" she appeared in the kitchen doorway, a five-foot-three-inch, one-hundred-and-two-pound ball of energy dressed in the yoga gear she wore ninety-nine percent of the time "—and today it feels like spring." She stopped short when she saw Terri standing there beside him. Then she smiled and said, "Well, hello there! I didn't know you were—"

Whatever she was going to say never made it out. Instead, she looked from him, to Terri, then back to him again. "Oh, my, it looks as if I've interrupted something."

He could see the wheels in her head spinning, and he knew exactly what she was thinking—that all the while they were posing as friends, he and Terri had been hitting the sheets together. Friends with benefits. And while he didn't care what she thought of him, he didn't want her to think Terri was like that. And he was pretty sure, by the crimson blossoming in Terri's cheeks, she was worried about the same thing.

Terri always said that his mom was the mom she should have had, and his mom said Terri was the third daughter she'd never had. Sometimes Nick could swear that if forced to ever choose, she might actually pick Terri over him.

"It's not what you think," he told his mom.

"Sweetheart, what you do in the privacy of your own home is none of my business."

"But we're not...I mean, we haven't been—"

His mom held up a hand. "No need to explain," she said, but underneath her blasé facade, he could see disappointment lurking there. And he was sure that it was directed as much at him as it was at Terri.

He turned to Terri and said, "So, should we tell her now?"

Terri looked over to his mom. "I don't know, what do you think?"

"Tell me what?" his mom asked.

"Well," Nick said. "She's going to find out eventually."

Terri grinned, enjoying this game as much as he was. There was no better way to drive his mom nuts than to make her think someone had a juicy secret and she'd been left out of the loop.

"I guess that's true," Terri said. "But are we ready to let the news out?"

"What news?" Though she was trying to sound nonchalant, he could see she was practically busting with curiosity.

"Because you know that as soon as we tell her, everyone will know."

"Nicky!" his mom scolded, even though they all knew it was true. She couldn't keep a secret to save her life. And oftentimes she told him things about family, or her "man-friends" as she called them, that he wished he could permanently wipe from his memory.

His mom folded her arms and pouted. "I know someone who's getting a big fat lump of coal in his stocking this year."

"Terri and I are getting married," Nick said.

"Married?"

"Yep."

"Really?"

"Yes, really."

She narrowed her eyes at him. "You're not just saying that because I caught you fooling around?"

He laughed. "We're *really* getting married."

His mom shrieked so loud he was sure the apartment below heard her through the industrial soundproofing. She scurried around the island to pull Terri—not him, but Terri—into a hug.

"Oh, honey! I'm so happy for you. I always hoped. You know I would never interfere, but I did hope."

Curiously, her idea of not interfering was telling him,

after meeting whatever girl he happened to be dating at the time, that "She was nice, but she wasn't Terri."

His mom held Terri at arm's length, tears shimmering in her eyes, looking as if it was the happiest moment of her entire life. Then she turned to Nick, the tears miraculously dried, and said, "It's about damn time."

Yep, she would definitely choose Terri over him.

"Have you set a date? And please don't tell me that this is going to be one of those ten-year engagements so that you can live together and not feel guilty. You know that you'll never hear the end of it from *Nonno*. He put your poor cousin Chrissy through hell when she moved in with David."

"We're getting married in two weeks."

She blinked. "Did you just say *two* weeks?"

"Yep."

She sucked in a breath and turned to Terri, asking in a hushed voice, even though there was no one around but them, "Are you pregnant?"

"No," Terri said, sounding incredibly patient under the circumstances. "I'm not pregnant."

Looking baffled, she shrugged and said, "Then what's the rush?"

"Neither of us sees any point in waiting," Terri said, shooting him a quick sideways glance filled with innuendo. "My plan has always been to be pregnant by the time I'm thirty, and I'm almost there."

"You want kids, Nicky?" his mom asked, beaming with joy.

"We want to try for a baby right away," he told her. "And we figured it would be best to get married first. We both prefer a small wedding, with a ceremony that's short and sweet. Immediate family and close friends *only*."

"You know that your father's family will have something to say about that."

"We'll videotape it and post it on YouTube," Nick said, earning him an elbow in the side from his fiancée. It also reminded him that they would need to hire a photographer, which then had him wondering if the studio that did the company's promotional shoots did weddings, too.

"Nicky, where's your laptop?" his mom asked.

"On my desk. Why?"

"With only two weeks, Terri and I need to start planning this thing right now. We have to pick out your colors and find a florist and I know just the place to get the cake." She exhaled a long-winded sigh. "There's *so much* to do!"

"But Mom…"

Ignoring Nick, she grabbed Terri by the arm and all but dragged her in the direction of Nick's office. Terri looked back over her shoulder, shrugging helplessly. So much for having a little premarital fun.

On the bright side, he doubted that after tonight they would be uncomfortable kissing and touching, so convincing his family that they were crazy about each other would be a breeze. And he was willing to bet that until he got her alone and into his bed, touching her again was all he would be able to think about.

Though Nick would have preferred to announce their engagement himself, his mom called his sisters, and his sisters called their cousins, and after that the news went viral. So it was no surprise when Tony and Rob cornered him as he was on his way to the test kitchen the next Monday morning.

"Is it true?" Rob asked.

"If you're referring to my engagement, then yes, it's true."

Tony gestured them into a room that wasn't much more than a glorified closet.

Oh, boy, here we go, Nick thought, doubting they were there for a friendly chat.

Boxes of old files lined metal shelves on either side and the air smelled musty. Tony switched on the light and shut the door behind them. "This seems awfully convenient, don't you think?"

Nick frowned, playing dumb. "What do you mean?"

"You know exactly what I mean."

"You've been friends with Terri for all these years," Rob said, "and you just happen to pick now to ask her to marry you?"

Nick leaned against a shelf and it shifted slightly under his weight. "What are you suggesting?"

"You know damn well what he's suggesting," Tony said. "And I don't think a marriage of convenience is what *Nonno* had in mind."

"I don't recall him ever saying that."

Rob shot him a look. "It was implied, and you know it. He wants us all to settle down and have big families. Lots of male heirs to carry on the Caroselli name."

"I love Terri," he said, which wasn't a lie. He just wasn't *in* love with her.

"Is she pregnant?" Rob asked.

With such a short engagement, he had the feeling he'd be getting that question a lot. "Not that it's any of your business, but no, she isn't. Not yet."

"Then why the big hurry to get hitched?" Tony said.

Though his family had many good qualities, they sure could be nosy.

"Again, not that it's *any* of your business, but we want

to start a family right away, and we want to be married first," he said, using the explanation Terri had given his mom last night, which was truly brilliant because none of it was untrue. They just left out a few pertinent facts.

Tony didn't look convinced. "Yeah, but two weeks is pretty fast, don't you think?"

"Terri is almost thirty and she has a ticking biological clock. And you know why *I'm* in a hurry."

Tony lowered his voice, even though they were alone. "Does she know about the money?"

Nick grinned. "What's the matter? Are you jealous that I'm going to get my cut of the money first?"

"Don't forget, it has to be a *male* heir," Rob said. "It could take more than one try. You could end up with three or four kids."

Of course, having a girl was a possibility, and whether or not they decided to ride it out and try again would be up to Terri.

"I think I speak for Rob when I say that we've always really liked Terri. And if either of us finds out you only married her so she'll have your offspring, and you hurt her, I will personally kick your ass."

Hurting her was definitely not on the agenda. They both knew exactly what they were getting into. What could go wrong?

"Honestly, Tony, I figured you would be making an announcement soon, too," Nick said. "You and Lucy have been together a long time now."

A nerve in Tony's jaw ticked. "It would have been a year in December."

"*Would* have been?" Rob asked.

"We split up."

"*When?*"

"Last week."

"Dude," Nick said. "Why didn't you say anything?"

Tony shrugged. "It didn't seem worth mentioning."

Nick couldn't say he was surprised. Lucy was never what anyone would consider a devoted girlfriend. In all the time they were together, she had been to no more than two or three family functions, and Tony rarely mentioned her. They seemed to lead very separate lives. "What happened?"

"I honestly don't know. I thought everything was fine, then I stopped by her place after work one night and she was gone. Her roommate said she moved back to Florida."

Rob shook his head in amazement. "Without saying a word?"

Tony shrugged again, but underneath the stoic facade, he was tense. Nick could feel it. "If there was a problem, she never mentioned it to me."

"I'm really sorry, man," Nick said.

"It's her loss."

Though Tony would never come right out and say it, Nick could tell that deep down he was hurting. But neither he nor Rob pushed the subject.

The door to the room opened and all three jumped like little boys caught playing with matches. A woman Nick didn't recognize stood in the open doorway, looking as surprised to see them as they were to see her. She was in her mid-forties, with short, stylish dark hair peppered with gray and striking blue eyes. She was very attractive for a woman her age, and there was something oddly familiar about her.

"I'm sorry, I didn't know anyone was in here," she said, looking nervously at them.

"It's okay," Tony said. "We were just talking."

She retreated a step. "I can come back."

"It's okay," Nick said, shooting his cousins a look. "We're finished."

"Nick, I don't think you've met Rose Goldwyn. Her mom, Phyllis, worked as *Nonno*'s secretary for years, up until he retired."

"For almost twenty years," Rose said.

Nick was struck with a distinct mental picture of a youngish, attractive woman seated outside *Nonno*'s office. That was why she looked familiar.

"I remember your mom," Nick said. "You look like her."

She smiled. "That's what everyone says."

"How is she doing?"

"Unfortunately mom passed away this September," Rose said. "Cancer."

"I'm so sorry. I remember that she was always smiling, and gave me and my sisters candy whenever we visited *Nonno* at his office."

"She always loved working here. Being here makes me feel a little closer to her."

"And we're happy to have you," Tony said.

"I heard this morning that you're getting married soon," she told Nick. "Congratulations."

"Thanks. You should come."

"Me?" she said, looking surprised.

"Sure. At Caroselli Chocolate, we like to think of our employees as extended family. I'll tell my fiancée to put you on the guest list. It's a week from this coming Saturday."

"I'll definitely be there," she said.

"Gentlemen, why don't we get out of her way," Tony said, nodding toward the door.

"Nice to have met you," Nick said, shaking her hand. They headed back down the hall in the direction of the kitchen, and when they turned the corner Nick asked, "When did we hire her?"

"A few weeks ago. We didn't actually need anyone, but because of the family history, they found a place for her in accounting. When she saw the condition of the file room, she offered to scan in the old files and take us completely digital."

"Correct me if I'm wrong," Nick said. "But isn't there a lot of sensitive information in there?"

Tony shrugged. "Mostly old financial records and employee files. Maybe some marketing materials. Nothing top secret."

"No old recipes?"

"Not that I know of. Why, do you think she's a spy?"

Corporate espionage certainly wasn't unheard of, especially with a world-renowned product like Caroselli Chocolate. "Doesn't hurt to be cautious."

Nick's cell phone rang and his mom's number popped up on the screen. "Sorry, I have to take this," he said, then told Tony, "If you need to talk…"

Tony nodded. Enough said.

Even if they weren't buying his story—because in all honesty, if the tables were turned he would have the same suspicions—Nick doubted they would rat him out to *Nonno*. Still, he planned to keep up the charade. If anyone else figured out that the marriage was a sham, it could definitely mean trouble.

"Hey, Mom, what's up?" he answered.

"White lilies or pink roses?"

"Excuse me?"

"Which do you prefer?" she said, sounding impatient, as if he should have known what she meant. "I'm at the florist with Terri and we can't decide between the lilies and the roses."

Not only did he not know the difference, he didn't care, either. "If you like them, why not pick both?"

"That's what I suggested, but she says it would be too expensive."

"And I told her that I didn't care what it costs. To get what she likes."

"Then you talk to her. She won't listen to me."

He heard muffled voices, then Terri came on the line. "Nick, the flowers are going to be really expensive."

He sighed. She was frugal to a fault. "It doesn't matter. Get whatever you want."

She lowered her voice. "For a fake wedding? I already feel horrible about this."

"Why?"

"Because your mom and your sisters are *so* excited. I feel like we're deceiving them."

"We are getting married, aren't we?"

"You know what I mean."

"Well, it's too late to back out now," Nick said.

There was a pause, and he wondered if she actually was reconsidering her decision. Then she said, "I guess you're right."

"And, Terri, get the flowers you want, regardless of the cost, okay? As long as we're married, what's mine is yours."

"Okay. I have to go, I'll call you later," she said. Then the line went dead.

They weren't doing anything wrong, so why did he get the feeling Terri still had doubts?

Five

Terri rummaged through her toiletries bag, checking off in her mind everything she would need for their honeymoon. When she was sure she had all the essentials, she zipped the bag and laid it in her suitcase. If she had forgotten something, she could pick it up when they got to the resort in Aruba.

She never realized just how much planning went into a wedding—even one as small as hers and Nick's—and thank goodness his mom and sisters were more than happy to tend to the details, leaving Terri time to finish up a high-profile web design job that was due to be completed while they were in the middle of their honeymoon. And since they already had to cut their trip short to be home in time for Thanksgiving, she doubted Nick would appreciate her bringing work with her. Which translated into five consecutive eighteen-hour days in front of the computer, until she was sure her eyes would start bleeding.

Nick had been developing a new product—one so top secret he couldn't even tell her about it—that they hoped to have in production before Easter, so he had been just as busy. Other than brief, nightly phone conversations to keep him up-to-date on the wedding progress, in which one or both of them started to doze off, their contact was minimal. They'd even had to skip their weekly Thursday dinner.

They hadn't discussed practicing for their wedding night since that evening in his kitchen, but it was never far from her mind, and she couldn't help but wonder if he'd been thinking about it, as well. Had he been having sex dreams about her, too? Fantasizing about their first time when he was supposed to be working?

When they finally did get a free night together the Wednesday before the wedding it was too late. According to her doctor it was best to refrain from sex at least five days before she ovulated, to keep Nick's sperm count high, which would make conception more likely. So after a short make-out session that only heightened the sexual tension, they decided it would be safer if they kept their hands to themselves until their wedding night. He helped her pack instead, which included dismantling her entire computer system so she could set up an office at his place. Then later, as they were relaxing by the fire, Nick got down on one knee and pretend-proposed—to give her the full experience, he'd said—but the four-carat, princess-cut diamond solitaire he slid on her ring finger was very real and stunningly beautiful, and hers to keep as a token of his affection even after they divorced.

While she thought it was a sweet gesture, it was a little heartbreaking that the best she could do in thirty years was a fake marriage proposal. But she knew he meant well. It wasn't his fault that she had lousy luck with men.

"All packed?" Nick asked from the bedroom doorway, and she turned to find him leaning casually against the jamb, thumbs hooked in the front pockets of his jeans.

"I think I may have over-packed," she said, tugging at the zipper in an effort to close the bulging case.

"You really think I'm going to let you wear clothes?" he said with one of those sizzling grins that made her heart flutter and her face hot. And though she probably wouldn't have noticed a couple weeks ago, in faded jeans that were ripped at the knees and a white T-shirt that enhanced his dark complexion, he looked sexy as hell. When they had first hatched this plan, the idea of sleeping with him wasn't just unusual, it really scared her. She didn't want their relationship to change. But then he'd kissed her, and touched her, and other than the fact that she was itching to get her hands on him and she couldn't wait to jump his bones, she didn't feel any differently about him than she had before. They were friends, and they were going to have sex—simple as that.

According to her temperature she should have started ovulating today, but the test she took this morning was negative. If the test had been positive, she didn't doubt that they would have consummated their marriage tonight, tradition be damned. And if she didn't start ovulating tomorrow? After two weeks of anticipating their first time making love, could they really hold out another day or two? She might have to say to hell with it and jump him, anyway.

"Anything you still need to do for tomorrow?" he asked. He'd already perfected his new recipe that would go through taste testing and marketing and whatever else they did with a new product, so they were free to spend the next five days relaxing and enjoying each other's company.

"I talked to your mom a couple hours ago and it sounds as if they have everything covered. I seriously don't know what I would have done without them. And I can't help feeling guilty."

"Why?"

"If they knew we're going to be getting divorced as soon as we have the baby, do you really think they would have spent all this time, and gone through all this trouble?"

"If we were getting married for real, who's to say it wouldn't end in divorce, anyway? There are no guarantees, Terri."

She knew that, but it still felt underhanded. Their current circumstance aside, she would never marry a man if she thought the relationship might end in divorce. Of course, would anyone? And there were definite advantages to being married, even if it was only pretend. It meant having someone to talk to without picking up the phone, and not eating dinner alone in front of the television watching *Seinfeld* reruns.

The best part, though, was that having Nick's baby meant always having someone to love—and someone to love her—unconditionally. Though her aunt had probably done her best raising Terri, she hadn't been much of a kid person. She'd never had children of her own, much less expected to have a great-niece she'd never even met dumped in her care. It had been a lonely way to grow up, but when the baby was born, Terri would never be lonely again. She would give her child all the love and affection her aunt had failed to show her. Terri would never make her child feel as if he was inconsequential. She wouldn't travel abroad for weeks at a time and leave him in the care of a nanny. She would be a good mom, and she hoped Nick would be a good dad. Either way, she had enough love to give for both of them.

"Are you nervous?" he asked.

She shrugged. "Should I be?"

"I hear that brides often are the day before their wedding."

Well, she wasn't a typical bride. "I'm just hoping everything goes well."

"Did my mom say what the final guest count will be?" Nick asked.

"Forty-eight."

"That's not bad. Maybe we'll get lucky and my dad won't show."

It broke her heart that Nick and his dad were so at odds. He didn't realize how lucky he was to have both his parents, even if they could be trying at times. She would have given anything to have her dad back. Her mom died when Terri was a baby, and it was harder to miss something she never really had, but she still regretted not getting to know her.

"I'm sure he'll behave," she told Nick. Or at least she *hoped* he would. His sister's wedding had been a disaster thanks to Nick's dad, Leo, who got into it with his ex-wife's date. The argument became so heated, shoves were exchanged, and though they never knew for sure who threw the first punch, fists began to fly. Eventually other family members from both sides of the wedding party had gotten into the scuffle, until it became a full-fledged brawl that resulted in a handful of arrests for drunk and disorderly behavior, several people requiring medical attention and an enormous bill for the damage from the banquet hall.

Never a dull moment in the Caroselli family.

But that had been more that thirteen years ago. His parents had been apart now for more years than they had been married, and had each wed and divorced again—in his dad's case twice. Terri would think that any issues they'd had back then would be resolved by now. Yet she couldn't deny worrying about what might happen if she was wrong.

"Everything will be perfect," she told him, hoping she sounded convincing.

"I hope so," Nick said. "I unpacked the last box of books and set up your computer system. I checked it and everything seems to be working correctly."

He had insisted that they get her moved in *before* the wedding, so the impending task wouldn't be in the back of their minds during their trip. She'd felt a little weird moving her things in before they were actually married. What if during their honeymoon something went terribly wrong? Sexually they seemed compatible enough, but suppose after four days in close quarters, they realized that they couldn't stand living together? She would have to fly home and move all her stuff back to her place.

That isn't going to happen, she told herself, but every now and then she thought about when they were roommates and doubt danced around the edge of her subconscious. There was also the question of sex. Not whether it would be good, but how often they would have it. Would they sleep together once, and hope she conceived, or the entire time she was ovulating? Would he be content to go an entire nine months without sex? The truth was that she liked sex. A lot. Even mediocre sex was better than none at all. And while she was perfectly capable of taking care of things herself, it was so much more fun to have a partner. But for her and Nick to have a full-blown affair would be a mistake. They had to keep this in perspective.

"Thanks for all your help today," she said, tugging the case off the bed so she could roll it out to the foyer. It weighed a ton.

"Let me get that," he said, taking it from her. He lifted it with little effort, then carried it to the entranceway and set it beside his own, which she noticed was half the size of hers and not nearly as stuffed. Maybe he really was expecting to spend the majority of their time naked.

This just kept getting better and better.

She looked over at the clock on the mantel, surprised to see that it was already after ten. "I should probably get home."

"Are you sure you don't want to sleep here?"

"In two hours it will be our wedding day, and it's bad luck for the groom to see the bride."

He gazed at her with tired eyes and a wry grin. "You don't really believe that."

Not really, but she'd be damned if she was taking any chances. "I think we should stick to tradition. Just in case."

He laughed. "And how is what we're doing *traditional?*"

"How many couples our age do you think still wait until their wedding night to consummate their relationship? That's a tradition."

"But we're only waiting because we *have* to. And I'd be happy to break that one right now."

Oh, man, so would she. But as much as she wanted to get him naked and put her hands all over him, she wanted to get pregnant even more, which meant they had to do this by the book.

"Everything that I need for tomorrow is at my place. It'll be easier if I stay there. But before I go, there is something I wanted to show you."

His brows rose. "Is it your breasts, because I'd love to see them."

She folded her arms and glared at him.

"That's a no, I guess."

"It's something I picked up at the doctor's office."

He followed into her bedroom and sat down beside her on the bed. She grabbed a manila folder off the nightstand and pulled out printed sheets, handing them to Nick.

He read the first line and his brows rose. "Methods for conceiving a boy?"

"I mentioned to the doctor that we were hoping for a boy and he gave me this. He said it in no way guarantees a baby boy, but there are some parents who swear by it. I highlighted the important parts."

The first couple pages were about ovulation and cervical conditions, and the differences in the mobility of the X and Y sperm.

"The male sperm are smaller and faster, but not as robust as their larger female counterparts," he read, giving her a sideways glance. "While trying to conceive a male, deep penetration from your partner will deposit the sperm closer to the cervix giving the quicker moving 'boy' sperm a head start to fertilizing the egg first. In addition, female orgasm is important as the contractions which accompany orgasm help move the sperm up and into the cervix. It also makes the vaginal environment more alkaline, which is favorable for the boy sperm." He turned to her, looking intrigued. "Deep penetration? How deep?"

"The next page has examples, actually."

Nick turned to the next page, which contained several vividly graphic illustrations depicting the positions they should use for the deepest penetration. His brows rose and he said, "Wow."

Along with a couple of tried-and-true positions, there were several that she was pretty sure only a contortionist could perform. And they had weird names like The Reverse Cowgirl and The Crab on its Back.

Nick narrowed his eyes, cocking his head to one side, then the other. "Huh, it looks like they're playing Twister."

"I admit some of them are a little...adventurous," she said. And not terribly romantic, if that's the mood they were going for. But they did look fun, and he had said himself that it should be fun. She liked to experiment and try new things, but maybe he was more conservative. Maybe his idea of fun was the missionary position. "They're just examples. I understand if you don't want to try them."

He looked at her as if she were nuts. "Are you kidding? Of *course* I want to try them."

Or maybe he *wasn't* conservative.

He pointed to one of the illustrations. "I like this, but do you really think you can get your legs over your head like that?"

She grinned. "I'm *very* flexible."

He cursed under his breath and handed the papers to her. "I think it would be best if I stopped looking at these. Because now I'm picturing you in all those positions."

What a coincidence, because so was she. She slid the papers back into the folder.

"I have to say, I'm a bit surprised by how open you are about this," he said.

"Why?"

"Over the years we've both made off-the-cuff comments about people we've dated, but we really never talked about our sex lives."

"Why do you think that is?"

"In my case, I consider it disrespectful to kiss and tell."

Good answer. While she was aware that he'd dated a lot of women, and *assumed* he'd slept with the majority of them, she really didn't have a clue how many. And frankly didn't want to know.

"In your case," he said, "I figured you were uncomfortable talking about sex."

"Repressed, you mean."

"Just...private. Like it probably took you a while to get to know someone before you would be comfortable being intimate with them. But then the other night, you were so..."

"Slutty?"

He shot her a look. *"Aggressive."*

"You don't like aggressive women?"

"Do I honestly strike you as the type who wouldn't like an aggressive woman?"

She wouldn't have thought so. But his perception of her, and reality, were two very different things.

"First you propositioned me," Nick said, "then you sat me down for a talk about sexual positions. And I'm not suggesting I don't like it. I think it's pretty obvious that I *do.* I'm just surprised. I thought I knew everything about you, but here's this side of you that I didn't even know existed."

It was odd, after all these years, there was still a part of her that he didn't know. But that was her own fault. "So you're seeing me differently than you did before?"

"A little, but in a good way. It makes me feel closer to you."

What she liked about their friendship was that it had always been very straightforward. There were no overblown expectations, and none of the games men and women played when they were physically involved. She didn't want that to change, though she couldn't deny that the idea of someone knowing her that well scared her a little. Especially now that sex was about to be part of the equation.

Six

Though he never thought he would see the day, Nick was a married man.

Legally, anyway.

He gazed down at the polished platinum band on the ring finger of his left hand. It was a brand, a warning to women that he was now taken, a tourniquet placed there to cut off the lifeblood of his single life. And while he'd expected that to bother him on some level, to make him feel caged or smothered, he actually felt okay about it. Maybe because he knew it was only temporary, or he was looking forward to collecting ten million dollars.

Or maybe he was looking forward to the honeymoon.

He'd received a text message from Terri at 6:00 a.m. this morning that read simply: The eagle has landed.

Which he knew was her way of saying that she was ovulating, and right on time.

Aside from the occasional random and fleeting fantasy,

he hadn't really thought about her in a sexual way since high school. The past two weeks, he had barely thought of much else, and after their conversation last night, it was *all* he'd thought about. Since the ceremony, he'd kept one eye on their guests—who were drinking champagne and expensive scotch, snacking on bacon-wrapped sea scallops, artichoke phyllo tartlets and gorgonzola risotto croquettes—and the other eye on the clock.

He heard Terri laugh, and turned to see her by the bar with his cousins, Megan and Elana. He rarely saw her in anything but casual clothes, but for the occasion she wore a calf-length, off-white dress made of some silky-soft material that flowed with her body every time she moved. Her long, dark hair was up in one of those styles that looked salon-perfect, yet messy at the same time.

His sister Jessica stepped up beside him and propped her hand on his shoulder. In three-inch heels, she was still a good eight inches shorter. She had their father's olive complexion and naturally curly hair, and took after their mother in height, but she had been struggling with her weight since she'd had her first of four babies. Right now she was on the heavy side, which usually meant she'd been stress eating, a pretty good indication that her marriage was once again on the rocks.

"She looks gorgeous," Jess said.

"Yes, she does," he agreed.

As if she sensed him watching, Terri looked over. She glanced up at the clock, then back at him and smiled, and he knew exactly what she was thinking. Soon they would be on their way to the airport, and after a five-hour flight, and a short limo ride, they would reach the resort.

It would be late by then, but he figured they could sleep on the flight, then spend the rest of the night making love in a variety of interesting ways.

"So, how does it feel?" Jess asked him.

"How does what feel?"

"To be a married man."

He shrugged. "So far so good."

"I never thought you would do it, but I'm glad you chose Terri."

"Me, too," he said. "And thank you again for everything. You and mom and Mags did an amazing job putting this all together."

With a satisfied smile, she gazed around the room. The decorations were simple yet elegant, and included both the lilies and the roses—even though Terri still insisted that it had been excessively expensive. And in lieu of the typical wedding band or DJ, they'd hired a string quartet.

"Considering you only gave us two weeks to plan it, I think so, too," she said.

"How are things with you and Eddie?"

Her smile slipped away. "Oh, you know, same ol' same ol'. We have good days and bad days. The marriage counseling seems to be helping. When I can get him to go."

Nick heard a screech, then Jessica's seven-year-old twin boys, Tommy and Alex, tore through the room like two wild animals, bumping furniture and plowing into guests.

Jess rolled her eyes and mumbled a curse. "Excuse me, I've got children to beat."

Nick knew that, physically, the worst she'd ever done was give them a quick love-tap to the back of the head, which was a long-running Caroselli family tradition. Only according to his father and his uncles, depending on what they'd done, and how angry they'd made *Nonni* Caroselli, hers were more like whacks, and were anything but loving. Nick still had a hard time picturing his *Nonni* as anything but sweet and gentle and unfailingly patient.

Terri crossed the room to where he stood, sliding her arm through his and hugging herself close to his side. He knew it was only for show, but he liked it. There was something nice about having the freedom to touch her, and be close to her, without having to worry that she would read into it, or take it the wrong way. She wouldn't smother him, or demand more than he was willing to give. He would call it friends with benefits, but that seemed to cheapen it somehow. What he and Terri had transcended a typical friendship. They were soul mates, but the platonic kind.

"So, I just had an interesting conversation with your cousins," she told him.

Uh-oh. "By *interesting* I take it you mean *not good*."

"Well, no one is questioning the validity of our wedding."

"That's good, right?"

"Yes, but only because apparently your *entire* family thinks I'm *pregnant*."

He sort of saw that one coming. "Did you tell them that you aren't?"

"Of course. And the reply I got was, 'Sure you aren't,' wink, wink, nudge, nudge."

"Let them think what they want, in eight months or so, when you don't give birth, they'll know you were telling the truth. Besides, I'm betting not everyone thinks it." His mom and sisters knew she wasn't, as did Rob and Tony.

"The limo will be here soon," she told him. "We should say our goodbyes so we can get upstairs and change."

Nick heard his dad's booming laugh, and turned to see that he and Nick's mom were standing together by the bay window talking. He muttered a curse under his breath.

The last time they had been in the same room, face-to-face, the evening had ended with a 9-1-1 call. And though they seemed to be playing nice, that could change in the span of a heartbeat if tempers flared. At least neither had brought a date, since that was what had set them off last time.

"Brace yourself," he told Terri. "I think there's going to be trouble."

"What's wrong?" Terri asked, following his line of vision until she spotted his parents.

Oh, hell.

Up until just then, their wedding had been perfect. So perfect that when *Nonno* walked her into the great room, and she saw everyone standing there looking so genuinely happy and willing to unconditionally welcome her into the family on a permanent basis, she had never felt so loved and accepted. If she wasn't careful, she could almost let herself believe it was real, that when Nick spoke his vows, he actually meant them. That when he promised to love and keep her, in sickness and in health, till death parted them, he was sincere. That the love in his eyes as he slipped the ring on her finger was genuine. If she never found Mr. Right, never married anyone for real, she still could say that she'd had the wedding of her dreams.

She didn't want his parents to ruin it by starting a brawl.

Her first instinct was to shove Nick over there to run interference, but then she noticed that his parents were both…*smiling.* Okay, that was a little weird.

"Is it me, or do they look as if they're actually getting along?" she said.

"Yeah, but for how long? All it will take is one snarky comment from either of them and the barbs will start flying."

Call her selfish, but she hoped they would wait until

she and Nick left for the airport before they decided to duke it out.

"Do you think I should go over there?" he asked, but before she could answer, his uncle, Tony Senior, joined his parents, then looked over at Nick and Terri and winked. Clearly they weren't the only ones concerned. And if anyone could keep hotheaded Leo Caroselli in line, it was his big brother.

"Thank you, Uncle Tony," Nick muttered under his breath, looking relieved. "Let's get the heck out of here. If there's going to be an explosion, I don't want to be around to see it."

Neither did she.

They made the rounds to aunts, uncles, cousins and friends from work, most of whom Terri knew on a first-name basis.

When they got to Tony and Rob, who were standing by the bar, Nick shook their hands and said, "Thank you for coming today."

"Yes, thank you," Terri said. "It meant so much to us to have you here."

"Wouldn't have missed it," Rob said, giving Terri a hug and a peck on the cheek. He smelled expensive, like scotch and cologne, and as always his suit was tailored to a perfect fit, his dark hair trimmed and neatly combed, and his nails buffed to a shine. She would bet her life that he probably got pedicures, too. He was so serious all the time, so...uptight. Even when they were kids, she had often wondered if he ever relaxed and had fun.

Tony was attractive in a dark, brooding sort of way, with his smoldering eyes and guarded smile. She'd never told Nick, but when they were in high school she'd had a short-lived crush on Tony. She was quite sure that, being six years her senior, he hadn't even noticed she was alive.

But now he kissed her cheek and said, "May you have a long and happy life together."

"We plan to." Terri smiled up at Nick and hugged herself close to his side, laying it on thick, since according to Nick, his cousins both had doubts the marriage was real.

"Think you can keep this guy in line?" Rob asked.

"The question is, can he keep *me* in line?"

Nick grinned. "I'll give it my best shot."

"I suppose you noticed your parents are talking," Tony said.

Nick shot a glance their way. "Yeah, but your dad seems to have it under control for now."

Terri could see that he was still nervous.

"I haven't seen your mom in a couple years," Rob said. "She looks great. Very…hip."

Nick's mom had always had her own unique style, so it was no surprise that she had substituted the typical conservative mother-of-the-groom dress for a long, flowing 1970s–style number that she could have picked up—and very likely *did*—at the vintage resale shop. In contrast, his dad looked like the typical executive in his thousand-dollar Italian suit. It's no wonder their marriage failed. Two people couldn't have been more different.

Terri glanced up at the clock and realized they were on the verge of running late. She gave Nick a nudge and said, "Our ride is going to be here soon."

"Again, gentlemen, thanks for coming," Nick said, and after another round of handshakes and hugs, with his arm firmly around her waist, they walked over to his parents. Tony Senior had left to stand by his wife, Sarah, leaving the two of them alone again.

"There's the happy couple," Nick's mom said with a bright smile as they approached.

"We're getting ready to leave," Nick told them. "We just wanted to say goodbye."

"Can't wait to get the honeymoon started, huh?" Nick's dad said, his booming voice making Terri cringe inwardly, as did his overly enthusiastic hug.

"Dad," Nick said in a tone that stated *back off.* But Leo ignored him. It wasn't that she disliked Nick's dad, she just didn't know him very well. And yes, he intimidated her a little, too. A far as she could tell, Nick had always been his polar opposite—at least in every way that mattered. Which is probably why they didn't get along.

"Thanks, Mr. Caroselli," she said when he let go.

He laughed heartily, drawing the attention of the entire room, and boomed, "You're my daughter now! Call me Dad!"

She actually preferred *Mr. Caroselli,* but didn't want to hurt his feelings.

Nick's mom—whom she had been calling Mom for the better part of twenty years—took Terri by her hands and squeezed them hard. "I know I've said this a dozen times in the past couple weeks, but I am so thrilled for the two of you. You are exactly what this guy needed." She smiled and gave Nick's jacket sleeve a playful tug. "Everyone in the family knew you were prefect for each other. I'm so happy that you both finally figured it out."

Terri braced herself against a jab of guilt. Though she liked everyone in Nick's family, his mom held a very special place in her heart. She had been the surrogate mother that Terri had desperately needed as a young woman.

She had taken Terri for her first bra, explained menstrual cycles and feminine hygiene products. And when Terri was finally asked out on her first date at the geriatric age of sixteen, Nick's mom had talked to her about the virtues of waiting, not necessarily for marriage, to have sex—she was far too progressive for that—but at least be until she was love. Then she took Terri to the clinic for birth control pills six months later when Terri decided she might take the leap sooner rather than later.

Nick's mom kissed him on the cheek, and gave Terri a hug, squeezing so hard it was difficult to breathe for a second. Her hugs were always warm and firm and full of love. She was so petite and fragile-looking, Terri was a little afraid to hug back too hard, for fear that she might crush her. But Terri had never known a tougher woman. Tough enough to stand up to—take no crap from—her brawny, loud and opinionated ex-husband. And when her second husband's dark side had emerged, and he took a swing at her, she swung right back. When all was said and done, she spent a few days in the hospital, but he spent those same days in jail with a broken nose and some deep scratch marks on his face so he would, as she phrased it, always have something to remember her by.

"Thank you so much for your help with the wedding," Terri said. "It was perfect. I couldn't have done it without you and Jess and Mags."

"Oh, honey, it was my pleasure. Any time you need my help, all you have to do is ask. And no pressure, but I throw a mean baby shower."

"We'll get right on that," Nick said, shooting Terri a glance that was so hot and steamy, she could practically feel it sizzle.

"So," Nick said, looking warily between his parents. "This is…different."

"What? That we're talking?" his mom asked.

"That you're not screaming at each other, and no fists are flying."

Another hearty laugh burst from his dad, propelling

his head back. "Water under the bridge, son. No hard feelings, right, Gena!"

Nick's mom smiled. "We were just saying that it's time we put the past behind us. That our whole problem was that we're just two very passionate people."

That was definitely one way to look at it. Although Terri always thought that is was simply that they didn't like each other.

Nick winced. "I have to admit, you're creeping me out a little."

"I would think you'd be happy," his mom said.

"Don't get me wrong. It's not that I don't want to see you bury the hatchet. I'm just afraid it's going to wind up protruding from someone's back."

"Not to worry, son," his dad assured him. "Everything is fine."

"Well, we've got to get upstairs and change," Nick told them. "Thanks again, Mom, for all your help."

"You two have fun on that honeymoon," his dad said with a wink that unsettled Terri more than a little bit.

His mom kissed and hugged them both. "Text me when you get there so I know you're safe. And have a good time."

Terri was forced to endure another overenthusiastic hug from his dad. As they were heading up the stairs Nick said, "Sorry about that. I know he can be obnoxious. And you don't have to call him Dad if you don't want to."

"He means well," she said. She didn't want to hurt his feelings, so she would probably force herself to call him Dad since it was only going to be for a short time.

They were running behind schedule, so Terri was thankful that she'd laid out her travel clothes ahead of time. There was nothing she hated more than being late, a virtue hammered into her by her aunt, who was intolerant of tardiness. Not that being on time had ever earned Terri any love and attention. In fact, back then, bad attention seemed favorable to being ignored, so she had been late a lot as a kid.

As they reached the top of the stairs and turned, a woman Terri had seen downstairs earlier, but hadn't yet met, was walking toward them from either the study or the master suite.

"Oh, thank goodness," she said, looking embarrassed. "I was looking for the bathroom but I must have made a wrong turn."

"It's the other way," Nick said, gesturing in that direction. "Second door on the left."

"Thanks. Your grandfather's house is really beautiful. My mother's descriptions don't do it justice."

"Terri, this is Rose," Nick said. "She was recently hired and her mom used to be *Nonno's* secretary."

"Pleasure to meet you," Terri said, shaking her hand. "Thanks for coming today."

"It was an honor to be invited," she said, but the smile she wore didn't quite reach her eyes. She seemed almost… nervous, as if they had caught her doing something underhanded.

"Well, we have a plane to catch," Nick said.

"Have a great honeymoon and a safe trip," she said, then headed swiftly down the stairs, bypassing the bathroom altogether. Call it intuition, or maybe she was just paranoid, but Terri had the feeling this woman was looking for something. And it wasn't the bathroom.

Nick gestured Terri into the spare bedroom where they'd left their things. She was about to voice her suspicions, but Nick closed the door and the next instant, he had her backed her against it, pinned with the weight of his body, his lips on hers.

Oh, man, could he kiss, and as much as she wanted to keep kissing him, they had to go. After a moment she laid her hands on his chest and gently pushed him away. "You know we don't have time."

"I know," he said. "But getting you naked is pretty much all I've thought about since last night."

His words thrilled her, and she liked the idea of him taking her right here, up against the door.

"Don't you think it would be nice if our first time wasn't rushed?" she asked. "And happened in bed?"

Nick gestured over his shoulder. "There's a bed right there."

"Nick—"

"Okay, okay," he said backing away. "But the second we get to Aruba, Mrs. Caroselli, you're mine."

Seven

Keeping his hands off Terri while she changed into jeans and a T-shirt, seeing her in her bra and panties, was the worst kind of torture, but Nick knew that if they were going to make their flight, the fooling around would have to wait. On sheer will he managed to restrain himself, but the image of her standing there mostly naked was emblazoned in his mind.

They arrived at the airport with an hour to spare, only to find their flight had been delayed due to a line of storms that spanned the entire southeast. As a result, they spent the next four hours stuck in the terminal playing solitaire on their phones, and sharing a less-than-gourmet meal at a fast food restaurant. When their flight was finally called, and they did get in the air, the ride was so bumpy neither of them could sleep. Terri sat beside him the entire five hours, her white-knuckled hold on his hand so tight that he had to let go every few minutes to shake the blood flow back into his fingers.

When they finally landed in Aruba, because of the flight delay, they had to wait another hour for their ride. By the time they reached the resort, and were shown to their suite—which was as luxurious as the description on the website, and about the only thing that had gone right so far—the sun was rising.

After a tour of all the amenities that at the moment Nick didn't give a damn about, he gave the bellboy a generous tip, hung the do not disturb sign on the door, then closed and locked it. "I thought that guy would *never* leave."

"It's official," Terri said, looking as beat as he was feeling. "I've been up for twenty-four hours."

So had he. He'd been known to pull all-nighters at work, then function reasonably well the next day. Maybe the stress of the past two weeks had finally caught up with him, or the miserable flight had worn him out, because his body was shutting down. Though he wouldn't have imagined it possible, he was too exhausted for sex. "Maybe we should take a nap."

Without hesitation Terri walked straight to the bedroom, yanked back the covers on the king-size bed and flopped facedown onto the sheet. She sighed and said in a sleepy voice, "Oh, that's nice."

Nick climbed in next to her and stretched out on his back, felt the mattress conform to his body as he relaxed.

Terri scooted close to him and cuddled up to his side, one arm draped across his chest, her breasts nestled against him. He'd been anticipating this day for two weeks, and now he was too damned tired to move.

"I want to jump you," Terri said, "but I don't have the energy."

"Me, neither," he said. "Can we at least sleep naked?"

She was quiet for a second, then sighed and said, "As nice as that sounds, I don't think I have the strength to take my clothes off."

He imagined all the movement getting undressed would require and said, "Come to think of it, neither do I."

"You know, I never imagined how stressful it could be planning a wedding, even with so much help. It was really nice, but I'm kinda glad it's over."

"I'm sorry if it wasn't your dream wedding."

"I was never one of those girls."

"What kind of girl?"

"The ones who start planning their wedding when they're barely out of diapers. I've always been more interested in finding the perfect *man*."

"Well, I'm sorry I couldn't be that, either." For a fleeting moment, he almost wished he could be. Because for him, she would be as close to the perfect woman as he would ever find. The problem was, he had no desire to be any woman's perfect man.

"You're helping me fulfill my dream of having a child," she said. "That's pretty huge."

If he wasn't so damned tired, he would be helping her fulfill that particular dream right now, but he could feel himself drifting off. She was still talking but the words weren't making it through the fog in his brain. He tried to keep his eyes open, but they refused to cooperate.

He finally gave in and let them close, and when he opened them again he was in bed alone. He looked at the time on his watch, surprised that he'd slept for over four hours.

He sat up, looking around the room, taking in the decor that he'd been too exhausted to notice earlier. The tropical theme was typical for the area, and could be a little too touristy for his taste, but here it was done well. He could smell the ocean, hear the water rushing up to meet the sand.

He rolled out of bed and went searching for Terri. Her bag lay open on the sofa, but she was nowhere in the suite. He opened the French doors that led out onto a small portico, then a narrow stretch of private beach. The air was warm but dry, and the sun so intense he had to shade his eyes. Guests sunned themselves in lawn chairs and swimmers dotted the crystal-clear blue water. Farther out was everything from sailboats and luxury yachts to commercial cruise ships.

He didn't see Terri anywhere, and figured she had probably gone for a walk, or maybe down to the pool.

He stepped back inside, thinking he would call her cell phone, until he noticed it sitting on the table by the couch.

He would take a shower instead, and if she wasn't back by the time he was finished, he would go looking for her.

He grabbed what he needed from his suitcase and stepped into the bathroom. The opened toiletries on the shower shelf, and wet towel hanging on the rack, told him that she'd already been there, and the remnants of moisture still clinging to the tile shower wall said it hadn't been that long ago. Too bad she hadn't woken him; they could have showered together.

He imagined how she would look, all slippery and wet, those long gorgeous legs wrapped around him, pressed against the shower wall. He wondered if that was a position that qualified as deep penetration. And decided right then that they would have to try it and find out.

He had just stepped out of the shower and was toweling off when he heard the suite door open.

"Nick!"

"In here." He fastened the towel around his waist and

exited the bathroom. Terri stood by the bed, dressed in nothing but a white bikini top that seemed to glow against her sun-kissed skin, and a pair of frayed, cutoff denim short shorts that showcased her slender legs, making them look a mile long. Her hair hung loose and damp around her shoulders, and the only makeup she wore was a touch of lip gloss.

It wasn't that he hadn't seen her dressed this way before. But those other times, he hadn't really *seen* her—not the way he was now. He had the feeling it was the same for her, because she hadn't peeled her eyes from his chest since he'd entered the room.

"Good nap?" she asked, her eyes finally lifting to his. They had a hazy quality that said she was already turned on. And knowing she was, thrust his libido into overdrive.

"Yeah. How long did you sleep?"

She shrugged. "A couple hours."

"You should have woken me."

"That's okay. I want you well rested."

He would ask why, but the way she was sizing him up, he was pretty sure he already knew. "So I guess this is the official start of our honeymoon."

"Then I guess it would be a good time to mention that I'm not wearing any underwear."

Damn. "What a coincidence, because neither am I."

Her gaze dropped from his chest to the towel and her tongue darted out to wet her lips. "Show me."

Terri watched as Nick gave the towel a quick tug, then let it drop to the floor. She looked him up and down, shaking her head. There was no getting around it—physically, the guy was perfect. "Wow. That is so not fair."

"What?"

"No one should look that good naked."

"And I'm all yours," he said, walking toward her with no modesty or shame, wearing that I'm-going-to-eat-you-alive look.

Her heart skipped a beat.

"Ready to make a baby?"

A baby. They were going to have sex, and try to make a baby.

Her heart gave a sudden, violent jerk as the reality of what she was doing, and who she was doing it with, hit her hard. Was she really ready for this? "We're going to make a baby," she said.

"Yep." He stopped in front of her and made a twirly gesture with his index finger. "Turn around."

"Together," she added, turning.

"That's the idea," he said, and with a quick tug, untied her bikini top. "Of course, we could do it alone, but that wouldn't be nearly as much fun."

Though she'd never been particularly shy about anyone seeing her naked, as her top fell away, she had to fight the urge to cross her arms over her breasts. What was wrong with her? For two weeks she'd been preparing herself for this, thinking about this exact moment over and over. When it came to sex, she always knew exactly what she wanted, and she'd never been shy about asking for it. So why, now, did she feel like a virgin, about to make love for the first time?

He must have sensed something was wrong, because he asked over her shoulder, "Are you still okay with this?"

"Of course," she said, but it was difficult to sound convincing when her voice was trembling.

"Are you sure? Because you sound a little nervous." His arms slid around her and cupped her breasts in his palms, easing her backward against his wide muscular chest. His skin was still warm and damp from his shower.

And even though it felt amazing, and she wanted more, her heart was in her throat.

"We could stop right now," he said.

Would he really? If she told him that she had changed her mind, that she was scared, he wouldn't be upset?

But she wouldn't get scared. Not about sex of all things. "I don't want to stop."

He ran the backs of his fingers slowly down her stomach to the edge of her shorts, and her skin quivered under his touch. One part of her was saying, *don't stop there,* while another said, *what do you think you're doing, pal? We're friends. You aren't supposed to touch me this way.*

"As long as we don't consummate the marriage," Nick said, tugging the snap open on her shorts, "we can still have it annulled."

She wasn't sure if he was serious or teasing her. What if he was serious? What would his family think? How would she explain that they'd gone through all that trouble planning a wedding for a marriage that lasted twenty-four hours?

"Terri?" he said, sounding unsure, his hands dropping away.

She turned, arms folded across her breasts. "What if I said I want to stop? That I thought we were making a mistake?"

He blinked, his expression a mix of confusion and surprise. "You're serious?"

She nodded.

He was quiet for several seconds, then said, "If you really don't want to do this, we won't."

"After everything we've been through the past couple weeks, you wouldn't be mad?"

"I would be disappointed, but our friendship comes first, always."

She could see that they weren't just words. He meant it. She wasn't just another woman he was sleeping with, or a convenient way to make ten million dollars. He really cared about her feelings. And she *knew* that. The truth was, this had nothing to do with him. This was about her insecurities.

When it came to relationships, love—or what she perceived love to be—always managed to elude her. And while sex, if she was lucky, was usually fun, she'd never felt the intense emotional connection that she was experiencing right now, with Nick. The *need* to be closer to him. She never *needed* anyone, and it scared her half to death. What if he let her down?

But this was Nick, the most important person in her life. The man she had barely gone a day or two without speaking with in the past two decades. He would *not* let her down. He wouldn't do anything to hurt her. And she refused to ruin what could very well be one of the most significant days in her entire life, just because she had intimacy issues. It was time she grew up, and let go of the past. Time she really trusted someone.

"Do you want to stop?" he asked. "We can."

"No. I don't want to stop."

He eyed her warily. "You're *sure*. Because once we get started, there's really no going back."

"I want this," she said, and she really did, even though she was scared. "I want *you*."

She dropped her arms, baring herself to him, and the hunger in his eyes as he raked his gaze over her made her heart beat faster.

"You had me worried there for a minute," he said. "Although I have to admit, I sort of like you this way."

"What way?"

"Not so confident. A little vulnerable."

Weirdly enough, she sort of liked it, too. She liked the idea of letting someone else take care of her for a change. Within reason, of course. She didn't want him getting the idea that she was a complete pushover.

She slid her arms around his neck and kissed him, then whispered in his ear, "Lay down."

"Now that's the Terri I know," he said with a grin, climbing into bed, watching as she shoved down her shorts and got in with him, straddling his thighs.

"You're so beautiful." He reached up, cupped her breasts in his palms, watched her nipples pull into tight points as he circled them with his thumbs. "I want to take my time, touch and kiss every inch of your body."

She smiled. "Well, if you have to…"

He pulled her against him, wrapped his arms around her and kissed her…and *kissed* her, disarming her with the rhythm of his tongue, his hands sliding across her skin, kissing and stroking away the last of her reservations, until she couldn't recall why she'd been afraid in the first place. And the more she responded, the bolder his explorations became. Still, she could tell he was taking his time, trying not to push too hard or too fast.

She just wanted to touch him—wanted *him*—and as close as he held her, as intimately as he touched her, it wasn't enough. She ached for something, but she wasn't sure what. She just knew she *needed* more. And though she preferred to have the upper hand, when Nick took control, rolling her over onto her back, she let him. Being so tall, logistics in bed could sometimes be a problem for her, but as he settled between her thighs, she and Nick were an ideal fit.

"That's better," he said, his weight pressing her into the mattress.

This was it, she thought, knowing that she would remember this moment for the rest of her life—the exact second when, with one slow deep thrust, they went from being friends to lovers.

She gazed down between them, to where their bodies were joined, thinking it was the most arousing, erotic thing she had ever seen. "Nick, we're making love," she said. "You're inside me."

He followed her gaze, transfixed for a moment, then he wrapped his arms around her and kissed her, started to move inside her.

She really thought she'd been prepared for this, that because they were friends, she could maintain a level of detachment, or objectivity. That it would be "fun" without those pesky feelings of affection to muddy things up. Boy, had she been wrong.

This wasn't supposed to change things, but deep down she knew they would never be quite the same.

"Deeper," she said. "You have to be deeper."

"I can't," he said, thrusting slow and steady, his shoulders tense, his eyes closed in concentration. "I'll lose it."

As it was, she was barely hanging on, and they needed to do this together, and not just so they would have a boy. She...*needed* it. "Nick, look at me."

He opened his eyes and looked down at her. The instant their eyes met, she was toast, and apparently so was he. With a growl, Nick grabbed her legs and hooked them over his shoulders, bending her in half, groaning as he thrust hard and deep, and her body went electric. It was shock and pleasure and perfection, and watching Nick's face, seeing him lose control, reaching their peak together, was the single most erotic experience of her life.

Afterward, Nick dropped his head against her shoulder, his forehead damp with perspiration. He was breathing hard. *"Wow."*

No kidding.

Nick eased her legs off his shoulders and she winced as her muscles, mostly the ones in her butt, screamed in protest. She stretched out her legs and her left cheek started to cramp up. She winced and said, "Ow! Charley horse!"

"Where?" Nick said, rolling off her.

"Left butt cheek."

"Turn over," he said, and when she did, he straddled her thighs and rubbed the knotted muscle, using his thumbs to really work it loose. "Better?"

"Hmm…that feels good," she said, as the pain subsided. She folded her arms around the pillow and tucked it under her head. "I'm going to have a talk with my personal trainer. All those hours spent in the gym, and I'm not nearly as flexible as I should be."

"I guess we'll just have to work on that," he said.

She sighed and closed her eyes. Though she was typically the one doing the pampering after sex, it was nice to be spoiled a little. Only problem was, she was getting a little *too* relaxed, to the point that her body was shutting down.

"Hey," Nick said. "I hope you're not falling asleep."

"Nope," she lied as the world started to go soft and fuzzy around her.

"We're not finished." He gave her a gentle shake. "Wake up."

"I'm awake," she mumbled, or at least she thought she did. It didn't matter because it was already too late. She gave in to the fatigue and drifted off to sleep.

Eight

Nick gave Terri a poke, then a harder poke, but it was useless. She was out cold.

He sighed. Wasn't it the *guy* who was supposed to roll over and fall asleep after sex? His plan had been for them to spend the entire day in bed, trying out many different positions. But he supposed he should be happy that they'd had sex at all.

It was a little difficult to reconcile the Terri from two weeks ago, who propositioned him in his kitchen, and the one who froze up today when he touched her. He wasn't sure what had happened, why she had suddenly gotten cold feet. At first he thought she was teasing him, playing coy, until he saw her face, then the metaphorical ball came out of left field and smacked him right between the eyes.

Was it something he did? Something he said? Did he hurt her feelings? Or was it something he'd had no control over whatsoever?

Damned if he knew.

She was ovulating, so her hormones were probably out of whack, and he knew from growing up in a house with three females, a hormonal woman could be unpredict-able—and at times downright scary. But weren't ovulat-ing women supposed to want sex more, not less?

Or was it possible that she didn't find him as appealing as she said she did? Was she so desperate to get pregnant, she would have told him anything?

Nah, that definitely wasn't it, because when they did finally get the ball rolling, it had been pretty freaking amazing. To put his hands all over that lithe, lean body, to feel those incredible legs wrapped around his waist. Over his shoulders.

Damn.

Even so, when he looked at her now, lying there, naked and gorgeous, she was still just *Terri,* his best friend. And other than wanting to put his hands all over her again, he couldn't say that he felt any differently about her now than he had yesterday. Which was exactly how he'd ex-pected to feel.

He assumed, since she would be ovulating for at least a few more days, there was no reason they couldn't have fun until then, or better yet, for the duration of their hon-eymoon. But he knew that when they returned to Chicago, they would go back to their previous platonic status. The truth was, they hadn't really talked about it. And that had probably been a mistake. But everything had happened in such a rush, they really hadn't had time.

Terri mumbled something in her sleep, then rolled over onto her side, curling up in a ball, as if she were chilled, so he tugged the covers up over her. As long as he'd known her she'd talked in her sleep. There were times, when they lived together, when he would pass by her room at night and hear her babbling incoherently. He would sometimes stop and listen, catch a random word here or there, but it usually didn't make any sense. If she seemed distressed, as if she were having a nightmare, which had happened often, he would push open her door a crack and peek in on her, just to make sure she was okay.

Sometimes he would hear her say his name, wondering what role he played in her dream. There were even times when he imagined crawling into bed with her. How would she react if he did? He never would have done it, though. She wanted the fairy-tale happy ending. A thing he could never give her, and after all the heartache in her life, she deserved to get exactly what she wanted. Even now he hated that she'd had to settle, that he couldn't give her everything her heart desired. But he just wasn't wired that way. Anyone he dated knew that from the start, although that didn't necessarily stop them from believing that they were different, that they would be the one he fell hopelessly in love with.

But Terri knew better. Didn't she?

He was sure she did. They had agreed this situation would be temporary. So why her mixed feelings today? Maybe it would be in everyone's best interest if they had a serious talk about the situation, and set some boundaries to prevent any future confusion. Just in case.

Nick's stomach growled, and he considered ringing for room service, but then he looked at the empty space beside Terri—and the cool sheets and fluffy pillows called out to him. She had said she wanted him well rested, hadn't she?

He stretched out beside her, his eyes feeling heavy the second his head hit the pillow. He rolled over on his side, draping an arm across her hip, wondering, as he drifted off to sleep, if it would be smooth sailing from here on out. Or would she have a change of heart again?

He got his answer when he woke from what he'd thought was an erotic dream. He opened his eyes, looked down at his crotch, and saw the top of Terri's head.

"I'm toast," Terri said.

She dropped face-first onto the sheets, sweaty and out of breath, and Nick fell on top of her, his weight crushing her against the mattress, making it hard to breathe. She was too exhausted to protest. They had been going at it, on and off, for three hours now, and she was ready for a break.

"Do you feel pregnant yet?" he asked, his voice muffled against her hair, which she was sure was probably a knotted mess.

"I think it takes a couple weeks for that part," she said. If she hadn't conceived the first three times they'd made love, she was pretty sure this last time would have done it. Their position, while slightly awkward at first, gave a whole new meaning to the phrase *deep penetration*. Plus, her thighs had gotten one hell of a workout.

She shifted under his weight, feeling light-headed from lack of oxygen. Gathering all her strength, she elbowed him in the ribs. "Hey, you're squishing me."

"Sorry," he said, rolling onto his back. "So, what do you want to do now?"

"Sleep?"

He looked over at her. *"Again?"*

Or not. "I don't know. What do people usually do on their honeymoon?"

He looked over at her and grinned, wiggling his eyebrows.

Good heavens, the man had stamina.

"Something besides intercourse," she said.

He thought about it for a minute, then said, "Oral sex?"

"Funny," she said giving him a playful poke, and he grinned.

"We could sit in the sand and watch the sunset," he said. "I hear they can be pretty spectacular."

"Which I suppose would necessitate me getting up and putting clothes on."

"Personally, I wouldn't mind if you went out there like this, but the other guests might object." He leaned over and kissed her shoulder. "If I could bring the sunset to you, I would."

Wow, that was probably one of the sweetest, most romantic things a man had ever said to her. She smiled and said, "I appreciate the thought."

"Come on," he said, giving her butt a playful smack as he rolled out of bed. "Get up."

She forced herself to stand and walk on jelly legs to the bathroom. It seemed strange that just this morning she'd been uncomfortable with him seeing her naked, and now it seemed perfectly natural. Not only had he seen it all, but there wasn't an inch that he hadn't touched in one way or another. When he told her that he thought sex should be fun, he wasn't kidding. And boy was he *good* at it. He seemed to take pleasure from giving pleasure, which she knew was rare.

She stepped into the bathroom and cringed at her reflection in the mirror. "I look like a beast. I need to do something with my hair."

He appeared in the doorway dressed in shorts and a T-shirt. "Yikes! You do look like a beast."

She glared at him.

"Kidding," he said, flashing her that disarming grin and planting a kiss on her cheek. "I'll meet you out there."

She wrestled a brush through the knots in her hair and brought it back into a ponytail. Not great, but it would suffice. She pulled a light sundress out of her bag and slipped it on, then stepped outside.

The air felt cooler. A gentle breeze rustled the the palm trees, their branches swaying in time like a tropical nature dance. And Nick was right about the sunset. Red-and-orange streaks above the horizon gave the illusion that the sky was on fire.

Nick was on a blanket in the sand a few yards from the water. He sat with his knees bent, his arms wrapped around them. She walked over and sat down beside him.

He smiled at her, nodding to the sky. "Nice, huh?"

"Beautiful."

He leaned back and looped an arm around her, and she rested her head against his shoulder. It felt…comfortable. She wondered if it would be okay to do this after they went home to Chicago, or if any sort of physical contact would be off limits.

"So," he said. "About earlier today…"

She cringed. It was embarrassing, really, the way she'd acted. And she still wasn't quite sure why. "Can we just forget about that?"

"I wanted to be sure that everything is okay now."

"It is, I promise." That should have been obvious the minute she woke him up from his nap, which was exactly why she'd done it. Well, that and he'd looked really good laying there naked.

"You were pretty freaked out," he said.

So apparently they *were* going to talk about it. "I know. I thought I had worked it all out in my head, but then you asked if I was ready to make a baby, and I guess I thought, *I don't know, am I?* It's a huge step. My entire life will change."

"And you were worried about it changing our relationship." It was a statement, not a question.

"That, too."

"Do you think it has?"

"Sort of. But not in a bad way."

"We never really talked about what will happen after the honeymoon."

Which she took to mean that they should talk about it now. "I just assumed we would go back to the way things were. Aside from the fact that we'll be living together, I mean. And, of course, your family will have to believe that we're...you know...*together*."

"So, no sex after the honeymoon?"

Was that disappointment she heard in his voice? Did he want to keep having sex? Or was she just imagining what she wanted to hear? Because she liked sleeping with him. Liked it too much for either of their own good.

"I think that would be best," she said. "Under the circumstances, an intimate relationship could get complicated. Don't you think? I know you don't want to settle down."

He thought about that for a minute, and her heart picked up speed. Was he going to say he wanted to keep sleeping with her? And how would she respond if he did? Even if she wanted it, too, would it be wise to tempt fate?

"You're right," he finally said. "I think it would be better if we went back to the way things were."

She was a little disappointed, but not surprised. And she was sure, when things went back to normal, they would be just as happy being friends.

"What if you don't get pregnant?" Nick asked.

"We try again next month. But not until I'm ovulating."

He nodded, as if that made sense to him, too. "And

if you don't get pregnant then? I mean, for all I know, I could be sterile."

"That's highly unlikely. And it would be fairly easy to determine."

"Even if we're both fine, it could still take months, right?"

"So what you're asking is, how long do we keep this up before we call it quits?"

He nodded.

"As long as we're both comfortable with it, I suppose."

An older couple, who looked to be close to Nick's parents' age, walked by, holding hands. Something about the way they moved together, the way they smiled at one another, made Terri think they had probably been married a long time, and were probably still deeply in love.

They smiled and said hello as they passed, and Terri actually felt a twinge of jealousy. As much as she wanted that for herself, and while most of her friends from college were already happily married and starting families, she had begun to believe that, for her, it would probably never happen. That maybe she was just meant for different things. The only thing she did know for sure was that until she became a mother, she would never feel truly complete. So whatever she had to do to make that happen, wasn't it worth the risk?

Terri woke the next morning to the sound of rain against the windows. Through the filmy curtains, she could see lightning slash across the sky. She glanced over her shoulder at Nick, who was curled up behind her, his arm draped across her hip. Though he was still asleep, certain parts were wide awake and pressed against her. She grabbed her phone and checked her weather app, which called for scattered thunderstorms all day. So much for their plans to rent a car and drive to Arikok National Park.

"Is that rain I hear?" Nick mumbled behind her.

"Yeah. It's supposed to rain on and off all day."

"Darn." Nick slid his arm around her, cupping her breast. "Guess we'll have to stay inside today."

She was sure they could find some indoor activity other than sex, but honestly, why would they want to? They only had a few more days before they went back to being just friends. Besides, newlyweds were supposed to have lots of sex on their honeymoon. Right?

They stayed in bed most of the day, and later that evening when the sky finally cleared, they showered together, then attended a party by the pool with the other resort guests. They played the role of the loving newlyweds, even though they would likely never see any of these people again.

They spent the following day in Arikok National Park. They rented a car, and quickly discovered that very few of the roads in Aruba were marked. They got lost a couple times, but it was worth the hassle when they got there.

Their first stop was Boca Prins, which they were told by another guest at the resort was the most beautiful thing in Aruba. With its beach cliffs, dunes and rocky shore, Terri had to agree. Although the sunset that first night definitely rated a close second.

They stopped for lunch at a local cantina, then drove to Fontein Cave and on to Guadirikiri Cave. Nick found her fear of the the lizards scurrying around incredibly amusing.

In the early evening they dropped off the car and took a taxi to downtown Oranjestad. They did a little shopping as they made their way to Fort Zoutman where they stopped to listen to a steel band and browsed the various local craft booths. They bought souvenirs for Nick's niece and nephews, and Terri found a pair of earrings she knew his mom would adore. She liked them so much she got a pair for herself, too.

Without street signs, it took a while to find the restaurant where they had made reservations for dinner, but the food was incredible. They ate and danced until they were exhausted, but not so much that it stopped them from making love when they got back to their room. After all, it was after their last night together.

Wednesday morning they packed and took a taxi to the airport for their flight home. They made it through security without a problem, found their gate and sat down to wait. That was when the reality of the situation hit home, and suddenly she wasn't ready to leave. Wasn't ready for this to be over.

The longer you wait, the harder it will be, she reminded herself. If they didn't end this now, what would they do? Continue on as lovers until the baby was born, or for the rest of their lives, yet never be in a committed relationship? She wasn't naive enough to believe that any friendship, even one as strong as theirs, could survive that. Besides, she wasn't quite ready to give up on the fairy tale. Finding Mr. Right, and living happily ever after.

But as Nick sat silently beside her, reading an issue of *Time* magazine, she couldn't help but wonder what he was thinking—if he was ready for this to be over or if he had regrets, too. Not that it would make a difference. So why was she obsessing about it?

Their flight was called right on time.

"I guess this is it," Nick said, stuffing the magazine into his carry-on bag. "The end of our honeymoon."

"I guess so." She grabbed her bag and started to stand, but Nick wrapped his hand around her arm.

"Terri...wait."

She sat back down, turning to him. "Is something wr—"

Nick hooked a hand behind her neck, pulled her to him and kissed her. It was slow and deep and bittersweet, and packed with so much raw emotion, she knew he was just as sorry to see this end. But like her, he knew they had no choice.

"Sorry," he said, closing his eyes and pressing his forehead to hers. "I just had to do that one more time."

They were doing the right thing, so why did she suddenly feel like crying? She was too choked up to say anything. If she tried, she would probably burst into tears, and where would that get them? It would just make him feel bad, and her feel stupid.

She pressed one last quick kiss to his lips, then stood and said, "We'd better go."

In the past five days she had grown used to touching and kissing Nick whenever she wanted. Now she would just have to get unused to it. Unless they were around his family, since it was necessary to keep up the ruse.

They boarded the plane, stored their bags and took their seats. With any luck, she was pregnant. She couldn't imagine how she wouldn't be, considering all the unprotected sex they'd been having. And though she almost hoped she hadn't conceived, so they could have honeymoon number two in about four weeks, she knew that dragging this out another month or so would only delay the inevitable. That it would probably be even harder next time.

After they were in the air, she reclined her seat and closed her eyes, pretending to sleep. It was easier than trying to make cheerful small talk, when she felt anything but happy. Nick kept himself amused reading his magazine. At some point she must have really fallen asleep, because suddenly Nick was nudging her and saying that the plane was going to land in a few minutes.

They didn't say much to each other during the miserably long wait in customs. What she wanted was to go back to her own place, curl up in her own bed and be miserable all by herself, but her home was at Nick's apartment now.

"You've been awfully quiet," Nick said, when they were in the car and heading for the city. "Is everything okay?"

She looked over at him and forced a smile. "Fine. I'm just tired. And not looking forward to all the work I have waiting for me."

It wasn't a total lie, but not exactly the truth, either.

"You will take tomorrow off, right?"

"Of course." She hadn't missed Thanksgiving with his family in years. "And maybe I'll do some Black Friday shopping with your mom."

"You're sure everything is okay?" he said.

"I'm sure." She pulled out her cell phone and checked her email. Nick took the hint and didn't ask any more questions.

The car dropped them off around dinnertime, and they rode the elevator up in silence. Though she continued to pretend that everything was fine, there was tension in the air, and she knew that he felt it, too.

She hated for their relationship to take this turn. As long as they had been friends, they had barely even had a fight.

It will just take a little time for things to go back to normal, she assured herself. After that, everything would be fine.

The elevator doors opened and sitting in the hallway outside the apartment door, a suitcase at her side, was

Jess, Nick's sister. She looked tired, and her eyes were red and puffy, as if she might have been crying.

"Hi, there," she said with a weak smile. "How was the honeymoon?"

Nine

"Jess, what are you doing here?" Nick asked, but considering the suitcase beside her, he could make an educated guess.

Jess pushed herself to her feet. "Can we go inside and talk?"

"Sure." He unlocked the door and they all rolled their luggage in. When everyone was inside, he shut the door and turned to his sister.

"Eddie and I are taking a break," she said. "Or, I am, anyway."

"What happened?"

"He blew off counseling for the third week in a row. Knowing I have that to look forward to, that it might make things better eventually, is the only thing that's kept me going the last couple months. He obviously doesn't feel the same way. So I left."

"What about the kids?"

"They're spending Thanksgiving in Indiana with Eddie's parents. They'll be there a week. I'm hoping we can work something out by the time they come back."

"What are you doing here?" Nick asked.

"Honestly, I couldn't bear the thought of staying alone in a hotel for the next week, and I know you guys have the extra bedroom." She smiled hopefully.

"What about Mom's place?"

"I didn't want to worry her. Also, I'd like to keep this quiet, and you know how she is. If she knows, *everyone* will know."

Nick was about to make up some excuse about him and Terri being newlyweds and needing their privacy, but before he could, Terri said, "Of course you can stay here."

"Thank you," Jess said, looking as if she were fighting tears. "You have no idea how much this means to me. And I won't get in the way, I promise."

"That's what family is for," Terri said, hugging her. "Just give me a few minutes to clear my clothes out of the spare room."

Jess frowned. "Why are your clothes in the spare room?"

Nick thought for sure Jess had her stumped with that one, but Terri didn't miss a beat.

"Have you ever looked in your brother's closet?" she asked Jess.

"If it looks anything like it did when he was a kid, I see your point."

"There's beer in the fridge," Nick said. "And the hard stuff is in the bar in my office. I'm going to help my wife."

Jess headed to the kitchen, while Nick and Terri walked to what was supposed to be her bedroom. When they were alone, he whispered, "You realize what you just did, right? You really think it's a good idea for us to share a bedroom? And a *bed?*"

"*No,* but what were we supposed to tell her? Sorry, you can't stay because *I'm* sleeping there? How would we explain *that?*"

If she had just given him a minute to think, he would have come up with something.

"Besides, it's only for a week." She opened the closet and grabbed an armful of clothes. "Do you have room for these in your closet?"

"I'll make room," he said, opening one of the drawers. Of course, with his rotten luck, it was full of lingerie. Damn. "And for the record, my closet looks nothing like it did in high school. Or college."

"I don't care how it looks, as long as it doesn't smell like sweaty sports gear."

He opened his mouth to argue, but realized it probably had smelled pretty awful.

"It doesn't," he said, as they dropped her clothes on his bed. "I keep my gym bag in the utility room behind the kitchen."

"I'll be sure to avoid it," she said, sounding annoyed.

She started to walk away and he grabbed her arm, turning her to face him. "Hey, this was *your* idea."

She looked as if she were about to say something snarky, then it seemed as if all the energy leaked out of her instead. "I know. I'm sorry. I just…I don't even know what's wrong. I'm tired, I guess."

"Just try to cut me a little slack, okay? This isn't easy for me, either."

"I know."

Maybe this scenario of pretending to be married wouldn't be quite as simple as they had imagined, or maybe they just needed a few days to adjust. One thing was certain—having Jess around wasn't going to make the transition any smoother.

They got the rest of Terri's clothes moved into his room and put away in his closet—which she made a point of observing was very tidy—and when they walked out to the kitchen, Jess had made them all dinner. After they ate, they put a movie on, but his sister clearly needed to vent. She alternated between complaining about Eddie and apologizing for complaining.

Around eleven Terri started yawning, which set him off. Once they got started it was a vicious cycle.

"You two must be exhausted from your trip, and here I am talking your heads off," Jess said.

"That's what family is for," Terri told her.

"Well, I'm going to stop whining now and let you two get to bed. And I'm sure I could benefit from a good night's sleep."

Nick was skeptical that she would get one, considering the state of her marriage, and he knew he and Terri wouldn't. Not if they were sleeping in the same bed.

Jess hugged them both good-night, thanked them again for letting her vent then went to bed. When Nick heard her bedroom door close, he turned to Terri. "I guess there's no point putting this off."

"I guess not."

He used the bathroom first, and while she took her turn, he undressed and climbed into bed. She came out wearing a nightshirt that hung to her knees, her hair loose. If it were still their honeymoon, she would be naked, and instead of climbing into the opposite side of the bed, she would be climbing on him.

"So how is this going to work?" she said, pulling the covers up to her waist.

He shrugged. "I stay on my side, you stay on yours."

She shot him a skeptical look. "You can do that?"

Did he have a choice? "It's a king-size bed. You won't even know I'm over here."

She still didn't look completely convinced, but she switched off her light, rolled away from him and pulled the covers over her shoulders.

"What, no kiss?" he said.

She glared at him over her shoulder.

"Kidding." The way she was acting one might have thought that letting his sister stay here had been *his* idea.

He turned off his light, settled onto his back and closed his eyes. He was physically exhausted, but his mind was moving about a million miles an hour, which could make for a very long and sleepless night. The last time he looked at the clock, it was one-thirty, but he must have drifted off because before he knew it, he heard Terri say his name, felt her nudging him awake. He didn't want to wake up; he was too content and comfortable curled up against something warm and soft. It took several seconds to realize that the thing he was curled up against was Terri, and she was looking at him over her shoulder.

"What are you doing on my side of the bed?" he asked. "I'm not."

He let go and sat up. Sure enough, he had invaded her side of the bed by several feet.

He scooted back onto his own side. "Sorry about that."

"Habit," she said. "Not a big deal."

"It won't happen again." He looked over at the clock and saw that it was only two-thirty. He rolled on his side facing away from her, determined to stay that way the rest of the night.

An hour later she woke him again. He was curled up against her like before, but this time his hand was up her nightshirt and cupped around her bare breast, and he was aroused. In fact, he was horny as hell.

"Um, Nick, maybe you should—"

He yanked his hand from inside her shirt and scooted away from her. "Why didn't you stop me?"

"Don't blame me," she snapped, rolling to face him. "I woke up that way."

He took a deep breath and blew it out. "Sorry, I didn't mean to accuse you."

She sat up. "This is not working. Maybe I should sleep on the floor, or in the bathtub."

"You know what the problem is," he said. "I usually sleep hugging a pillow, but you're lying on it, so I'm hugging you instead."

"Do you have a pillow you could hug instead of me?"

He switched on the light and started to get up, then turned back to her and said, "You may want to look the other way."

Her brows rose. "You don't want me to see you in your pajamas?"

"I wouldn't care if I were wearing any."

Her mouth fell open in surprise. "You're *naked?*"

He shrugged. "I've always slept naked. I don't even own pajamas."

"You own underwear, right? I mean, I've seen you wear it."

He sighed. "I'll put some on."

He hadn't slept with anything on since he was fifteen, but he would just have to get used to it, he supposed.

Terri turned away from him as he got out of bed. But he could swear, as he walked to the closet, he could feel her eyes on him, specifically his ass. He tugged on a pair of boxer briefs, grabbed a pillow from the top shelf, switched off the light and walked back to bed. "Got it."

"And you're not naked?"

"Nope." He climbed into bed. With the skivvies on, he was instantly uncomfortable. Fantastic.

"Well, good night," she said.

"Good night." Though it probably wouldn't be. He curled up with the pillow between them, and must have fallen asleep pretty quickly, because when Terri nudged him awake the next time, it felt like minutes, when in reality a couple hours had passed.

"Nick, you're doing it *again*."

She was right. His arms were around her, his hand was back up her shirt and he was as aroused as he had been the last time.

"Sorry," he said scooting away for a third time, feeling around for the pillow. When he couldn't find it, he asked Terri, "Where did the pillow go?"

"I don't have it," she snapped.

And she was clearly annoyed with him. Not that he could blame her. He switched on the light, and Terri grumbled in protest, covering her head with her pillow. As his eyes adjusted, he looked all around the room and discovered it lying on the floor at the foot of the bed. He must have lobbed it in his sleep. "There it is."

"Awesome."

"I said I was sorry." He threw off the covers in frustration and shoved himself out of bed.

"Nick!"

He turned to her and realized she was staring at the front of his...well, not his underwear, because at some point he'd apparently taken it off. And she was getting an eyeful.

She sat up in bed. "You said you put underwear on."

"I did! I guess I must have taken them off again." He pulled back the covers, and sure enough, there they were, kicked down near the foot of the bed. He grabbed them and said, "Got 'em."

"This is ridiculous," Terri said.

"I'll put them on."

"And what, *staple* them in place?"

Preferably no. "No need to get vicious. And keep your voice down. Jess is going to hear you."

"Do you have any idea what it's like to wake up with someone fondling you?"

It sounded pretty good to him, but by her tone, he was guessing that she disagreed.

"Look, I'm doing my best."

She sat there in silence for a few seconds, just staring at him—mostly at his crotch—then shook her head and said, "Screw it."

He thought her next move would be to grab her pillow and a blanket and charge off to sleep in the tub. Instead, she pulled her nightshirt over her head and said, "Get over here."

Confused, he opened his mouth to speak, then closed it again.

"What are you waiting for?" she asked, tugging off her panties.

"But...I thought we weren't supposed to—"

"Hurry, before I change my mind."

He climbed into bed, and she pushed him onto his back, straddling his thighs.

"For the record, this is it," she said. "This is the last time. Got it?"

"Got it," he said, then sucked in a breath as she leaned over and took him in her mouth.

This pretending to be crazy-in-love thing was going to be harder than Terri originally thought, and maybe telling Jess she could stay hadn't been such a hot idea, after all. Nick was curled around her again and sound asleep—from the waist up, at least. Sure, it never should have happened, and they were only delaying the inevitable, but Terri couldn't deny that after she had jumped him, she had slept like a baby the rest of the night. Which technically hadn't been all that long, since it was eight now and they hadn't gone to sleep until five. But it was definitely going to be the last time, even if that meant sleeping on the couch. She would come up with some plausible excuse to tell Jess. Like Nick snored, or...well, she would think of *something*.

She slipped from under Nick's arm and got out of bed. He grumbled for a second, then went right back to sleep. She grabbed her nightshirt from the floor and pulled it over her head, then shrugged into her robe. As she walked to the kitchen, the aroma of freshly brewed coffee met her halfway there.

Jess was sitting on one of the bar stools, dressed in what Nick referred to as her mom-clothes—cotton pants and an oversize men's button-up shirt—sipping coffee and staring off into space, looking tired and sad.

"Good morning," Terri said.

Jess looked over at her and smiled brightly. "Happy Thanksgiving! I made coffee."

"It smells delicious." She crossed the room to the coffeepot and pulled down a cup from the cupboard.

"It's a fresh pot. I made the first when I got up and it was getting a little funky. I forget that not everyone is on a mom schedule."

Terri poured herself a cup and added a pinch of sugar. "When did you get up?"

"Five-thirty."

"Yikes! The earliest I ever manage to get up is seven, but usually it's closer to eight-thirty."

"One of the benefits of working from home," Jess said. "You roll out of bed and you're there. Of course, that will change when you have kids. For the first year, you'll barely sleep at all." She grinned and added, "Not that you seemed to be getting much sleep last night."

"I'm sorry if we woke you."

"Don't apologize. You're newlyweds. It's what you're supposed to do. And I'd be lying if I said I wasn't jealous. I can barely remember the last time Eddie and I had sex. And the last time we had really *good* sex? It's been ages."

Terri couldn't fathom why Jess would stay married if things were so bad. It's no wonder Nick and Maggs were so against tying the knot. First their parents' marriage ended in disaster, now Jess was turning it into a family tradition.

"So, speaking of kids," Jess said. "I noticed you didn't drink wine with dinner last night. Does that mean…?"

"I'm pregnant?" She shrugged. "I hope so, but I won't know for sure for another week and a half. I'm trying to be cautious just in case. Which means I shouldn't be drinking coffee, either, I guess."

"Or you could start drinking decaf. I think it still has a trace of caffeine, though."

Well, then, this would be her last cup of real coffee, she supposed. She would have to remember to pick up some decaf tomorrow.

Terri sat beside her. "So, how are you doing?"

She shrugged. "Everything about this situation sucks. I'm just so tired of dealing with it. Sometimes I wonder if it's even worth fighting anymore. It's not fair to the kids." She laid a hand on Terri's arm. "But you and Nick, you're different. I've never known two people who were more suited for each other. I mean, look how long you've been friends."

If only that were true. If only they loved each other that way. Because if things could stay just like they were now, she could imagine them being happy together. Of course, there was the slight problem of Nick not wanting to be married. "That doesn't necessarily mean we were meant to be married."

"Terri, are you having second thoughts?" Jess whispered, looking concerned.

"No, of course not. I'm just trying to be realistic."

"As long as you don't let your fears get in the way of your happiness. If you convince yourself it won't work, it won't."

"Was there a time when your marriage was good?"

"The first couple years were great. I mean, we had our disagreements, no marriage is perfect, but we were both happy."

"What do you think went wrong?"

"Marriage takes hard work. I think we got lazy. Between work and raising the kids, we forgot how to be a couple. Does that make sense?"

"I think so." Being friends could be a lot of work, too. It required compromise and patience. Twenty-year friendships, the ones as close as hers and Nicks, were probably as rare as twenty-year marriages. In a way it sort of was like a marriage. Just without the sex. And honestly, they probably talked as much as or more than most married couples.

"Plus, we have a few other issues…" Jess started to say, but her brother walked into the kitchen, and she clammed up. Did that mean it was something she didn't want him to know about?

Dressed in jeans and nothing else, his hair mussed

from sleep, Nick looked adorable. But when didn't he, really? Too bad last night—or, technically, this morning—had been the absolute last time.

"Good morning ladies," he said, sounding way too cheerful. He gave his sister a peck on the cheek, then scooped Terri into his arms, dipped her back and planted a slow, deep kiss on her.

"*Ugh,* get a room," Jess teased, walking to the sink to rinse her cup.

Nick grinned and winked at Terri. "How did you sleep, sweetheart?"

She flashed him a stern look, and gave him a not-so-gentle shove. It was one thing to be affectionate with each other, and quite another for him to molest her in front of his sister. Okay, maybe she did hesitate a few seconds before she pushed him away. But still...

He walked around the island to pour himself a cup of coffee. "So, when are we supposed to be at Mom's?"

"Eleven," Jess said, sticking her cup in the dishwasher. "Dinner is at five at *Nonno*'s. Would you mind if I tag along with you guys? I get the feeling the only way I'll make it through dinner this year is by consuming copious amounts of alcohol."

"I won't be drinking," Terri said. "I can be the designated driver."

"So I can get hammered, too?" Nick said with a hopeful grin.

She shrugged. "If you really want to."

It didn't matter to her. She'd known guys who were quiet, brooding drunks, reckless and irresponsible drunks, and downright mean drunks. The worst she'd seen Nick do when he was really hammered is act a little goofy and get super-affectionate. Although not creepy, molester affectionate. He would just hug her a lot, and tell her repeatedly what a good friend she was, and how much he loved her.

"In fact, why don't we start right now?" Nick said. "We have almost a case of champagne left over from the wedding. I could go for a mimosa."

"Oh, that sounds good!" Jess said, rubbing her hands together. "I'll get the glasses and the orange juice."

"I'll open the champagne," Nick said.

And I'll watch, Terri thought, feeling left out. But she knew that having a baby would take sacrifice, and as far as sacrifices go, this one would be minor. And if nothing else, it would be an interesting day.

Ten

Nick's sister Maggie called asking if she could tag along with them to their mom's and then *Nonno's*. She drove over to Nick's place and they all piled into his Mercedes, with Terri driving, since Nick and Jess had already polished off a bottle and a half of champagne. And it was barely ten-thirty.

Nick's mom served Bellinis with brunch, a traditional Italian cocktail made up of white peach puree and prosecco, an Italian sparkling white wine.

Terri lost track of how many pitchers the four of them consumed, but by the time they left for *Nonno's* house, no one was feeling any pain. At one point Nick leaned over, touched her cheek, gazed at her with a sappy smile and bloodshot eyes and said, "I love you, Terri."

He was rewarded with two exaggerated *awww's* from the backseat. They didn't realize he meant that he loved her as a friend.

"I love you, too," she said, taking his hand and placing it back on his side of the front seat so she could concentrate on the road. But before she could pull away, he grabbed her hand and held it tight.

"No, I mean I *really* love you."

She pried herself free and patted his hand. "I really love you, too."

"It's not fair," Maggie whined from the backseat. "I want what you guys have."

"Me, too," Jess said.

Nick looked over his shoulder at his sisters. "You've told me a hundred times that you would never *ever* get married, Mags."

"And you actually *believed* me? Every woman wants to be married, moron. I only say I don't to spare myself the humiliation of being thirty-three and still single."

"I'm going to be forty," Jess said.

Nick scoffed. "In *three* years."

"Besides," Maggie said. "You're *married.*"

"But for how long? I keep telling myself things will change, but they never do." Jess sniffed. "He's not even trying anymore."

"So leave him," Maggie said. "You deserve to be happy."

"I can't."

"Why not?" Nick said.

"There are certain things I'm not willing to give up, like private school for the kids. And do you have any idea how much sports programs cost? I would have to take out a third mortgage."

"Third?" Nick said, and Terri didn't have to see his face to know that he was frowning. She glanced back at Jess in the rearview mirror, and it looked as if all the color had drained from her face. Was she going to be sick?

"You know, forget I said anything," Jess said.

"No," Nick said. "That house was a wedding gift, there shouldn't be a mortgage."

"Can we please drop it?" she asked, sounding nervous.

Nick apparently didn't want to drop it. "Why did you mortgage the house, Jess?"

"Raising a family is expensive."

"You both make good money, and you have your trust to fall back on."

When she didn't answer him, Nick said, "Jess, you do still have your trust? Right?"

"I have enough socked away to put the kids through college, but I won't touch that."

"And the rest?" Mags asked.

Her cheeks crimson, she said, "Gone. It's all gone."

"Where?" Nick demanded.

She hesitated, then said, "Bad investments."

"What kind of investments?"

"Well, it depends on the season. Football, basketball…"

Nick cursed again and leaned back against the headrest, staring straight ahead. "Jessica, why didn't you *tell* someone?"

Jess sniffed again. "It was humiliating. I hoped that the marriage counseling might help him work that out, too, but whenever the subject comes up, he gets furious and denies that there's a problem. That's why he stopped going. I'm not sure what to do now. If there's anything I *can* do."

"Maybe he just needs a little persuasion," Nick said.

Jess paled even more. "What are you going to do?"

"He works for Caroselli Chocolate, and if he wants to keep his job, he'll play by our rules. Either he goes to Gamblers Anonymous, or he's out of a job."

"And then where will the kids and I be? We have so much debt, we're barely hanging on as it is."

"If Eddie won't take care of you," Nick said, his jaw tense, "then the family will."

Terri felt so awful for Jess. She couldn't even imagine what it would be like if someone lost all of her money, and to something as careless as gambling. She wouldn't even waste her money on a dollar scratch-off ticket.

The mood in the car was pretty somber the rest of the way to *Nonno's*, and when they got there, Nick and his sisters went straight to the bar. Wishing she could join them, Terri said hello to everyone—trying not to cringe as Nick's dad gave her one of those cloying hugs—then headed upstairs to use the bathroom. As she reached the top of the stairs, she heard voices coming from *Nonno's* study. A man and a woman. Curious, she stopped to listen, but couldn't make out what was being said, only that they both were angry.

She stepped closer, straining to hear, even though it was none of her business. My God, she really was becoming a Caroselli.

"We have to tell him," the man was saying.

The woman, sounding desperate, said, "But we agreed never to say a word."

"He deserves to know the truth."

"No, I won't do that to him."

"I've kept this secret, but I can't do it anymore. The guilt is eating away at me. Either you tell him or I will."

"Demitrio, wait!"

The doorknob turned and Terri gasped, ducking into the spare bedroom, her heart pounding. She hid behind the door and watched through the crack as Nick's Uncle Demitrio, Rob's dad, marched out, followed a second later by Tony's mom, Sarah. Terri had no clue what they could possibly be fighting about, though she could draw several conclusions from the small snippet of conversation she'd heard. Then again, she could be completely misconstruing the conversation. She could ask Nick, but if he told Tony and Rob what she'd heard, and they confronted their parents, all hell could break loose and she didn't want to be responsible.

When she was sure they were both gone, she used the bathroom, then rushed back downstairs before anyone could miss her.

Elana, Tony's younger sister, stopped her in the great room just outside the dining room door. She had been labeled the family genius after graduating high school at sixteen. She earned her masters five years later and passed the CPA exam shortly after that. She worked in the international tax department of Caroselli Chocolate, and according to Nick, would probably take over as CFO some day.

"So, how are you?" she said, shooting a not-so-subtle glance at Terri's stomach.

"Good." *And by the way, I think your mom is having an affair with your uncle.*

"How was Aruba?"

"A lot of fun. I'd like to go back some time." Maybe after the divorce, she and Nick and the baby could go for a non-honeymoon there.

"I see you don't have a drink. Can I get you something?"

"Thanks, but I can't. I'm the designated driver tonight."

"Oh, right," she said, but Terri doubted she believed her. "I did notice that your husband and his sisters seemed to get an early start this Thanksgiving."

By the time the evening was over, the rest of the family would be hammered, too. It was a Caroselli holiday tradition.

She heard Nick laugh, and spotted him, drink in hand, leaning on the bar. "Excuse me, Elana, I need to have a word with my husband."

Elana grinned. "Sure. Say hi to Gena for me when you see her."

"I will," she said, heading in Nick's direction.

"Hey," Nick said, smiling brightly as she approached. "Where'd ya go?"

"Bathroom. How are you?"

"Just standin' here holdin' up the bar," he said, his speech slightly slurred.

"You mean, the bar is holding you up?"

He nodded, his head wobbly on his neck. "Pretty much."

"Maybe you should give me that," she said, gesturing to his drink, and he handed it over without argument. She set it on the bar, out of his reach. "Why don't we go sit down? Before you fall over."

"You know, that's probably a good idea."

He hooked an arm around her neck and she led him to the sofa. If she hadn't been so tall and fit, he probably would have gone down a couple times and taken her with him.

She got him seated on the couch, but before she could sit beside him, he pulled her down onto his lap instead.

"Nick!"

He just grinned, and whispered in her ear, "Everyone needs to believe we're crazy in love, remember?"

Yes, but there were limits.

She thought about what she'd heard upstairs, and curiosity got the best of her. She doubted Nick would remember much of this night, anyway. "So, what's the deal with your Uncle Demitrio and Aunt Sarah?"

"What do you mean?" he asked, fiddling with the bottom edge of her dress.

She moved his hand to the sofa cushion instead. "I saw them talking and it sounded...strained."

"Well, they do have a history."

"They do?"

He laid his hand on her stocking-clad knee instead. "I never told you?"

If he had, she couldn't recall. "Not that I remember."

"They used to date."

Uh-oh. "Seriously?"

"In high school, I think." His hand began a slow slide upward, under the hem of her dress. "But Demitrio enlisted, and dumped Sarah, then Sarah fell in love with Tony instead."

And in light of what she'd heard upstairs, Terri would say it was pretty likely that Sarah and Demitrio had rekindled their romance. But since it was none of her business, she would keep it to herself.

Nick's roaming hand was now pushing the boundaries of decency. She intercepted it halfway up her thigh.

"Behave yourself," she said, and before he had the chance to do it again, Nick's dad announced that dinner was served.

She assumed she would be relatively safe at the dinner table, but thanks to a tablecloth that hung just low enough, she spent a good part of her meal defending herself against his sneak attacks.

She knew he could be affectionate when he drank, but she'd never known him to be so...hands-on. Of course, the last time she saw him this drunk, they weren't sleeping together. And as much as it annoyed her, she liked it, too.

The food was amazing, and the wine flowed freely, but Terri was able to limit Nick to two glasses. Unfortunately no one was keeping an eye on Jess and Mags, and by the time people started to leave for home, they were so toasted, Terri needed the assistance of Rob—whom she'd never seen even the slightest bit intoxicated—to get the girls in the car, and wondered how the hell she would get them in the building and up to Nick's apartment.

When everyone was buckled in and the doors were closed, Rob asked, "You want me to follow you and help get them upstairs?"

"Would you?" she said. "That would be so awesome. Unless his building has a flat-bed cart I could borrow, it would probably take me half the night to get them up to the apartment."

And just in case she had conceived, it would probably be better if she didn't lift anything too heavy.

"Let me go get Tony and we'll swing by Nick's—I mean, your apartment, on our way to Tony's place."

When she climbed in the car, Nick looked over at her, that goofy grin on his face. "Thanks for being designated driver."

"No problem." She buckled up and started the engine.

He let his head fall back against the rest and loll to one side. "I had a lot to drink today."

"You certainly did."

"Are you mad?"

"A little jealous maybe, but not mad."

He closed his eyes as she pulled away from the curb. They hadn't even made it to the corner when, his eyes still closed, he said, "Are we there yet?"

She laughed. "I bet you were a riot as a kid."

He grinned, and must have fallen asleep after that, because he didn't make another sound all the way to his building. Rob and Tony were a few minutes behind her, and they each took a sister while Terri led Nick—who thankfully was able to walk with little assistance—upstairs.

Rob and Tony got the girls into the guest room, and Terri got Nick undressed—all the way down to nothing because he would end up that way eventually—and into bed.

She leaned down to give him a kiss on the cheek, and discovered that even intoxicated, he was lightening fast. He looped an arm around her neck and pulled her in for a kiss. A long, slow, deep one. He smelled so good, felt so nice, that she let it go on longer than she should have.

He looked up at her, brushing her hair back and tucking it behind her ears. "Do you have any idea how long I've wanted to do this?"

"Um, since the last time you kissed me?"

"For years," he said. "And I wanted to do more than just kiss you."

"Uh-huh." That was definitely the alcohol talking.

"Terri, I mean it. When we lived together, I would meet girls and bring them home—"

"I *remember*."

"But what you didn't know was that when I was with them, I would be wishing it was you."

Her heart took a dive, then shot back up into her throat. "Come on, Nick. You did not."

"No, I did," he said, his eyes so earnest she could swear he was actually telling the truth. But he couldn't be. He was only saying it to soften her up, so she would sleep with him again.

"If you wanted me so much, why didn't you tell me?"

"I should have," he said. "I wish I would have."

"No you don't." He was clearly confusing her with some other woman.

"Yes, I *do*. In the car, when I said I love you, I meant it."

"Of course you did. We're best friends. I love you, too."

"No. I mean, I *really* love you."

In a way she wanted to believe it, but she knew it was just the alcohol making him sentimental. She'd seen it happen before.

"I think I always knew it was inevitable," he said, his eyelids heavy.

"What was inevitable?"

"That we would end up together. And Jess was right, we are perfect for each other. Now I can't believe we didn't figure it out a long time ago. Maybe we just weren't ready."

"You should go to sleep," she said. "We can talk about it in the morning, okay?"

"Okay," he said, letting his arm drop from around her neck, his eyelids sinking closed.

She stood up, knowing that despite what she'd said, this was not a conversation they would be continuing. She doubted he would recall a single word of it.

She switched off the light and walked out to the kitchen. Rob sat on one of the bar stools, drinking a bottled water. Tony had helped himself to a beer and leaned against the fridge drinking it.

"What a night," Terri said, sitting beside Rob. "Thanks for helping me."

"So, what's going on?" Tony asked.

"What do you mean?"

"I've seen Nick and his sisters get pretty drunk, but never all of them at the same time. Is everything okay with Gena?"

"Gena is fine."

"Does it have something to do with Eddie not showing up for dinner?"

"Maybe you should ask Jess about that."

"So it is about Eddie," Rob said.

"I can't really say one way or the other." But they would find out soon enough if Nick followed through and gave Eddie that ultimatum.

"You know," Rob said. "You'll never survive in this family if you don't learn to gossip."

Your dad is sleeping with Tony's mom, she wanted to say. How was that for gossip? "Let's just say it's been a tough day for everyone."

"Everything okay with you and Nick?"

"Great. We're great."

"He mentioned that you guys wanted to start a family right away," Rob said. "And I noticed that all you drank tonight was water."

He and half a dozen other people had noticed. And inquired.

"A preemptive precaution," she said.

She was under the distinct impression that she was being pumped for information. Had Rob and Tony agreed to *Nonno's* offer, too? Would they be making engagement announcements of their own? And if they did, would this turn into some sort of race to the finish line?

Eleven

Last night's overindulgence had taken its toll, and when Terri returned home around eleven the next morning after a few hours of Black Friday shopping with Nick's mom, she encountered a gruesome scene. Jess and Mags were sacked out in the living room, the curtains drawn, the television off, looking miserable.

"Good morning," Terri said, setting her packages on the floor beside the door so she could take off her coat.

"Not really," Jess said weakly, a compress on her forehead, eyes bloodshot and puffy. "Is it physically possible for a head to explode? Because it feels like mine might."

"I don't think so," Terri said.

"Shhh," Maggie scolded. The previous night's makeup was smeared around her eyes, giving her a raccoon appearance. "Do you two really have to talk so loud?"

"Did you guys take anything?" Terri asked, and both nodded. "Are you drinking lots of water?"

"Yes, Mom," Maggie said.

"Hey, I've gotta practice on someone. Where's Nick?"

"He got up and took some ibuprofen then went back to bed," Jess said.

"How did he look?"

"Have you seen the movie *Zombieland?*" Maggie asked.

"That bad, huh?" Terri had been a little jealous last night to be the odd man out, but in the aftermath, she was glad she hadn't been able to let loose. "I'd better go check on him."

Terri hung her coat in the closet and gathered up the other three coats that had been dumped in various spots throughout the room and hung them up, too. Then she tiptoed into the bedroom. The blinds were closed, all the lights off and Nick was sprawled out diagonally, facedown on the mattress naked, as if he had collapsed there and didn't have the strength to move another inch. He may have been hungover, but he sure did look good.

There were two empty water bottles on the bedside table—so at least he'd had the good sense to hydrate—and a pair of jogging pants on the floor. She picked them up and draped them across the foot of the bed. During their honeymoon, he'd been pretty good about picking up after himself. He left an occasional wet towel on the floor, or whiskers in the sink, but so far he was nowhere near as bad as he used to be.

She was about to turn around and leave, when Nick mumbled, "What time is it?"

"After eleven. You okay?"

He lifted his head and gazed up at her. Only one eyelid was raised, as if he just didn't have the energy to open them both. The eye she could see was so puffy and redrimmed it almost hurt to look at it. "What do you think?"

"Is there anything I can get you?"

"A gun?"

She laughed. "Anything else?"

He sighed and dropped his head down. "Another bottle of water? And a promise that you'll never let me do that again. I must be getting old, because I'm not bouncing back like I used to in college."

"That happens, I guess." The last time she'd overdone it with a pitcher of margaritas, she'd paid severely the following day. "I'll be right back."

She walked to the kitchen for his water, stopping to ask his sisters if they wanted one, too. They both moan-mumbled an affirmative, and she grabbed an armful from the fridge. She set two beside each sister, then returned to the bedroom, where Nick was actually sitting up in bed. She sat on the edge of the mattress beside him and handed over the water.

"Thanks." She watched his Adam's apple bob, the muscles in his neck flexing as he guzzled down the first bottle in one long gulp. He set the second one on the bedside table for later. He sighed, letting his head rest against the headboard. "Thanks."

"No problem."

"How are the girls doing?"

"In a little better shape than you, but not by much."

"Thanks for taking care of us last night."

"You would have done the same for me. And if I recall correctly, you have a time or two."

He slipped down, flat on his back. "Like the time in high school when you broke up with Tommy Malone and you went a little crazy with the peach Schnapps."

"It was peppermint Schnapps, and I didn't break up with him. He dumped me for Alicia Silberman because

I wouldn't put out. And apparently she was more than happy to."

"I did offer to kick his ass for you."

She smiled at the memory. He would have done it, too. "He wasn't worth the trouble."

"So when did you finally do it?" he said.

Confused, she asked, "Do what?"

"Have sex."

The question took her aback. Not that she was ashamed of her past—not all of it, anyway—but it just wasn't something they had ever talked about. "Why do you want to know?"

"Just curious. I was a junior in high school."

"I heard," she said. "With Beth Evans, in her bedroom when her parents were both at work."

"Who told you?"

"I overheard Tony and Rob talking about it a couple years ago. And, of course, there were rumors around school at the time." Which she had rarely put any stock in, but apparently this time they were right. "I hear you gave quite the performance."

Nick laughed. "Not exactly. I was so nervous I couldn't get her bra unhooked, and the actual sex lasted about thirteen seconds."

"That's not the way Rob tells it. He said that you said you had her begging for more."

"I may have exaggerated a tiny bit," he said with a grin. "Sexual prowess is very important to a teenage boy. The truth is, it was a humiliating experience."

"Well, if it's any consolation, you've perfected your methods since then."

He laughed. "Thanks. When was your first time?"

She cringed. "It's embarrassing."

"Why?"

"Because it was so…cliché."

"Tell me it wasn't a teacher."

It was her turn to laugh. "Of course not! It was the night of senior prom."

"You're right, that is cliché." He paused, then said, "Wait a minute, you went to prom with that guy from the math club. Eugene…something."

"Eugene Spenser."

"Wasn't he kind of a…*geek?*"

"A little, but so was I." And that *geek* had moves that she later realized put most college guys to shame. He actually *did* have her begging for more.

"I don't remember you dating him."

"Um…I don't think you could call what we did dating, per se."

His brows rose. "What *would* you call it?"

"Occasionally we would…hook up."

The brows rose higher. *"Hook up?"*

"You know, have sex."

He sat up again, his hangover temporarily forgotten. "Really?"

"Yes, really."

"You would just…have sex. No relationship, no commitment?"

She nodded. "That's about it."

"Were there *other* guys that you 'hooked up' with?"

"A few."

"But they weren't boyfriends."

"They were friends, but not boyfriends."

"And you had sex with them?"

"I had sex with them," she said, unsure why he found the scenario so unbelievable. "What can I say, I liked sex."

"So did I, but…"

"But it's supposedly different for you?"

"Yes."

"Why? Because you're a guy? Or because you were madly in love with every girl you slept with? I'm recalling the parade of females in and out of your room when we lived together, and I can't say I remember seeing the same face more than once or twice." Which made her think about what he'd said last night. How he would be with a girl but think of Terri. But he'd been so drunk he probably hadn't meant it. He probably didn't even know what he was saying.

"Well, we know you didn't sleep with *all* your friends," he said.

"Not any of my girlfriends, if that's what you mean. Although one did invite me into a three-way with her boyfriend once, and I might have if the guy hadn't been such a creep."

"You never slept with *me,* either."

She shrugged. "You never asked."

His brows perked up again. "If I had, would you?"

At first she thought he was teasing, but his eyes said that he was serious. Had he really wanted to sleep with her back then? Were those not just the ramblings of a drunk man last night? And did she really want to know? It's not as if they had any kind of future as a couple now, so what difference did it make?

"No. Our friendship was too important to me."

"And theirs weren't?"

"Not like ours. For me sex was…I don't know. I guess it made me feel in control. And special in a way. Definitive proof of how much my aunt screwed me up, I guess."

"Do you still feel that way?" he asked, looking intrigued.

"No, not anymore." She also didn't like the direction

this conversation was taking. It was too...*something*. "Well, I should let you get back to sleep."

"I'm feeling better now. I think I'll take a shower instead."

"Are you hungry? I could pick up lunch."

"Something light, maybe? I have soup in the pantry."

As long as he didn't mind her potentially burning down the building. "Sure. It'll be ready when you're done."

"Unless you'd like to join me," he said, wiggling his brows.

"I thought you were hungover."

"Not *that* hungover."

She couldn't help but laugh, and wonder if there would ever be a time before the divorce when he would stop coming on to her. Or a time when she stopped wanting to say yes. "Well, the answer is no."

He shrugged. "Thought it couldn't hurt to ask."

He rolled out of bed, deliciously naked, and walked to the bathroom. Terri watched him, trying her best not to drool, noting that he'd left the door wide-open.

It was a good thing he didn't realize how little persuasion it would take to change her mind, or she would be joining him.

She heard the shower turn on and before she could even be tempted, or think how good he looked naked and soapy, how his body felt all slippery and warm against hers, she hightailed it to the kitchen, stopping to see if Jess and Mags were hungry.

"I can barely choke down saltines," Jess said. "But thanks."

"I'll pass, too," Maggie said. "I need to get home soon, anyway."

"Let me know if you change your minds."

In the kitchen she opened the door to the walk-in pantry, which was remarkably well organized for a man who used to leave his canned goods in the bag on the kitchen table for days after a trip to the store.

There was an entire shelf dedicated to a dozen brands and types of soup, but she didn't have a clue what he would prefer. Under normal circumstances he liked tomato, but she wondered if that might upset his stomach.

Crap. That meant she would have to go ask him. She would stand outside the bathroom and shout to him, so she wouldn't have to see him through the clear glass shower doors. It would just be easier that way.

That was exactly what she did, and Nick did in fact want tomato, but as she started to walk away, he called, "Hey, Terri, would you grab a washcloth from the cabinet for me?"

Crap.

"Okay," she called. She planned to just throw it over the top of the shower door and run, but before she could, Nick swung open the door. Of course he was wet and soapy, and sexy as hell.

She held out the cloth to him, but he grabbed her wrist instead, tugging her, fully clothed, into the shower and under the hot spray.

"Nick!" she shrieked, trying to pull away, but he wouldn't let go.

"Well, gosh," he said as water saturated her sweatshirt and jeans, her hair. "Looks like now you *need* a shower."

Water leaked out of her hair and into her eyes and her wet clothes were weighing her down. She wanted to be mad, wanted to feel like slugging him, but all she could manage was a laugh.

His hand slid down to cup her behind and he wedged one thigh intimately between hers. A moan slipped out and her head tilted against the tile, giving Nick access to her throat, which he promptly began to devour.

She should be telling him no right now, but damn it, she didn't *want* to. Instead, she said, "This is it," as he kissed his way upward, nibbling the shell of her ear. "This is the *last* time."

He pulled back, eyes black with desire. "Take off your clothes."

Terri pushed her cart through the produce section of the grocery store, dropping in the items on the list Nick had put together last night for her. When she lived alone, she did the majority of her shopping in the frozen food section, so the gourmet meals Nick had been making every night were pretty cool. They also made up for the fact that, although he'd improved a lot, Nick hadn't quite lost all his slob tendencies. He often left newspapers or magazines on the coffee table, or dirty clothes on the bedroom floor, and he never seemed to clean up after himself after using the bathroom in the morning.

But those things didn't bother her nearly as much as they used to. She'd been living alone for a long time now. She had worried that having someone there, having to share her space, would feel suffocating. She also thought she would miss her condo, but that wasn't the case at all. Now that Jess was back home trying again to work out things with Eddie, and Terri had the guest room to herself, she missed sleeping with Nick. And not just the sex, which they agreed would stop the day she moved out of his bedroom.

She'd grown awfully fond of cuddling, and she missed lying in bed with him and just talking. There were so many little things that she realized she'd taken for granted. And she was starting to get the feeling that she and Nick just being roommates might not cut it anymore. Maybe she wanted more than that.

But then she always reminded herself that despite what she wanted, Nick was perfectly content with his life just the way it was. He didn't want to be tied down. And whatever happened with the baby, she knew that in time she would be okay with that. Knowing he was her best friend, and always would be, would be enough for her.

She hoped.

Right now, though, as the date approached when she could take a pregnancy test, she became more and more obsessed about it. She was ultra aware of any changes in her body, any signs of pregnancy. She would check her reflection to see if she was glowing, poke her breasts to see if they were tender. She even started eating foods that she'd read could aggravate morning sickness to encourage signs of pregnancy, but so far, nothing. She tried not to let it discourage her, but she was nervous. Suppose it didn't work this month, or the next, or the next? What if she discovered that she couldn't get pregnant?

Every time her thoughts started to wander in that direction, she forced herself to stay positive. Even if the first try was unsuccessful, it didn't mean the second would be, too. She just had to be patient.

On her way to the dairy section, Terri passed the aisle with the feminine products, and took a detour. Though she had to wait until after her period was late to test, it couldn't hurt to buy it a few days early.

She grabbed the most expensive one—thinking it would be the most accurate—and read the back, both stunned and excited to see that the test could be performed as soon as four days before her period was due, which coincidentally was today.

Heart jumping in her chest, she tossed the box in the

cart. She hurried through the rest of her shopping and paid for her groceries, so nervous and excited she barely recalled the drive home. She forced herself to wait until she got all the groceries upstairs and put away, then she opened the box and pulled out the instruction leaflet.

Her excitement fizzled when she read the line that said to take it with the first urine of the day, which she had flushed away almost *ten* hours ago. *Damn.* If she wanted an accurate reading, she had no choice but to wait until tomorrow morning.

She stuck the test in the cabinet in her bathroom and tried to forget about it, but failed miserably.

Later that night, after the tenth time of not hearing Nick ask her a question or make a comment about the movie that she wasn't really watching, he seemed to realize something was up.

"Is everything okay?" he said. "It's like you're here, but you're not really here."

At least if she told him, she wouldn't be the only one crawling out of her skin. "When I was at the grocery store today, I went down the feminine products aisle."

He frowned. "Is this something I really want to know about?"

She rolled her eyes. "The pregnancy test aisle, Nick."

"I thought we had to wait until your period was due to test."

"So did I, but the directions said you can take the test as early as four days before your period is due."

"When is that?"

"Today. But it was too late in the day, so I can't test until tomorrow morning."

"How early?" he asked, and it was hard to tell if he was excited, or nervous, or really didn't give a crap. His face gave nothing away.

"As soon as I wake up."

He pulled his phone from his pocket and started to fiddle with it.

"What are you doing?" she asked.

"I'm setting my alarm for tomorrow morning."

"For what time?"

He looked at her and grinned. "Five."

Twelve

Nick paced outside the bathroom door, like an expectant father waiting for news on the birth of his child, not the result of a pregnancy test. And what was taking so long? Weren't they supposed to give results in minutes?

The door opened and Terri stepped out, still in her pajamas.

"Well?" he said.

"It's still marinating. I just couldn't stand there watching it."

"How much longer?"

She looked at her watch. "Three minutes."

"Don't worry," he said. "It'll be positive."

"You realize that if it is, that's it. For the rest of your life, it will no longer be about you, you'll always have this person depending on you."

Hadn't they been over this before? Why did he get the feeling she was trying to scare him? Or maybe she was the one who was scared. She had to carry the baby for nine months. The one making the most sacrifices. "I'm ready," he assured her. "And I'm here for you. For whatever you need. No matter what the results are."

"Meaning, if it's negative, you still want to try again?"

"Terri, I'm in this for the long haul."

"For the money."

"Don't you think it's a little late in the game to be questioning my motives?"

She sighed. "You're right. I'm sorry. I guess I'm just nervous."

"We're in this together. If you don't trust me—"

"I *do*. I don't know what my problem is. Maybe I'm hormonal."

She looked at her watch again and said, "It's time."

Here we go.

She took a step into the bathroom, then stopped. "I can't do it. I'm too nervous. You look at it."

"What am I looking for?"

"A plus sign is positive, a minus sign negative."

"Okay, here goes." He stepped into the bathroom and picked up the little stick off the counter. He turned it over and looked in the indicator window for a plus sign…

Damn.

"Well?" she asked hopefully from the doorway.

Damn, damn, damn.

He looked up at her and shook his head, watched her face fall. "Are you sure you did it right?"

"Yes, I'm sure. It's not as if it's the only one I've ever taken."

That surprised him. "Really?"

She nodded. "I had a few scares in college."

"Why didn't you tell me?"

"What difference does it make?" she snapped, and he realized he was being insensitive.

"I'm sorry. Come here." He held out his arms and she walked into them, laying her head against his chest. "Is there anything I can do?"

She shook her head. "The directions do say that I could get a false negative taking the test this early. They say to try again the day my period is due."

"So, you could still be pregnant?"

"There's only a twelve percent chance, so more than likely, I'm not."

"Twelve percent is better than zero percent. You'll test again Tuesday and then we'll know for sure."

Nick tried to keep a positive attitude all day, tried to keep Terri's mind off anything having to do with pregnancy or babies, did everything he could think of to cheer her up. He made her favorite dinner, but she only picked at it. Then he suggested they rent the chick flick she'd been bugging him about, but she looked so lost in thought, she probably hadn't absorbed the plot.

They said good-night at eleven, and it was almost midnight when Terri appeared in Nick's bedroom doorway. "Nick? Are you awake?" she whispered.

He sat up. "Yeah. Are you okay?"

She took a few steps into the room. "Can't sleep. Would it be okay, just for tonight, if I sleep with you? And I mean, actually sleep, not—"

"I get it." He pulled back the covers on the opposite side of the bed. "Hop in."

She climbed in beside him and he laid back down, facing her.

"Sorry about this," she said, shivering and burrowing under the covers. It did seem particularly cold, which meant she had probably been messing with the thermostat again. At her condo, she kept her thermostat at a balmy sixty-three degrees. He could swear she'd been an eskimo in a past life. Or a reptile.

"Don't apologize. I like sleeping with you."

"For years I've managed to fall asleep just fine on my own," she said, sounding disgusted with herself.

"It's been a rough couple of days. You don't have to go through everything alone. We're in this together, remember?"

"For now, but there could come a time when you're not around, and I have to be able to stand on my own two feet."

"Where is it you think I'm going?"

"Like my aunt used to tell me, if you don't let yourself depend on people, they can't let you down."

Nick could hardly believe she'd just said that, that she would even *think* it. He knew she had trust issues but if she really believed that, her insecurities ran much deeper that he had ever imagined.

"Have I ever let you down?"

"No."

Why did he get the feeling there was an unspoken "not yet" tacked to the end of that sentence? "So, who? Your parents? I really don't imagine they *wanted* to die."

"No, but they did."

He sighed. "Terri—"

"I'm not wallowing in self-pity or looking for sympathy. It just is what it is. You never know what might happen, so it's important to be self-sufficient. That's all I'm saying."

"''Tis better to have loved and lost, than never to have loved at all,'" he said.

"And after you lose someone, see if you still believe that."

She said it not as if it were a possibility, but a predestined event. He didn't even know how to respond to that, what he could say to change her mind. If it was even possible to change it. But the real question, the thing he needed to decide first was, did he want to?

Unfortunately, they never needed that second pregnancy test. Terri started her period Monday morning. As long as he'd known her, he'd seen her cry maybe four or five times total, but when she called him that morning at work to tell him the bad news, she was beside herself.

"Do you want me to come home?"

"No," she said with a sniff, her voice unsteady. "I'm being stupid. I knew this would happen, but I guess I was still hoping. I shouldn't be this upset."

"It's okay to be upset. I'm disappointed, too. But we try again in a couple weeks, right?"

"You're sure you want to do that?"

"Of course I'm sure." He'd only told her that a dozen times since Saturday morning. Was she really worried that he would back out, or was *she* the one having second thoughts? "But you realize that means being stuck living with me for an extra month. Think you can handle that?"

"Well," she said, her tone lighter, "you are pretty high maintenance."

He laughed, because they both knew that couldn't be farther from the truth. "So, when does act two start?"

"I haven't figured that out yet. I'll do that later today."

"What sounds good for dinner? I'll make or pick up anything you want."

She paused for a second, then said, "Pizza. From the little Italian place around the corner. With ham, mushrooms and little hairy fish."

"Pizza it is," he said. He heard a knock and looked

up to see his dad standing in the open doorway, and he didn't look happy. Nick's gut reaction was to immediately wonder what he'd done this time, but that was just a holdover from his childhood. He didn't answer to his father anymore, and sometimes he still forgot that, still got that sinking feeling when he walked into the room.

"Terri, I have to let you go."

"Okay. I…I love you."

"I love you, too. I'll see you around seven." He hung up and looked over at his dad. "What's up?"

"Sorry to interrupt, but I need to talk to you."

"Come in."

He stepped inside and shut the door behind him, which was probably not a good sign.

He took a seat across from Nick, his brow furrowed, far from the happy-go-lucky facade he wore most of the time. Even if he were smiling now, it would have no bearing on what he'd be doing five minutes from now. He had a hair-trigger temper and could turn on a dime.

"I've noticed something lately," he said. "And I thought maybe you knew what was going on. That Tony and Rob may have mentioned something."

"About what?"

"Your Uncle Tony and Uncle Demitrio."

"No, they haven't said anything. Why? Is something wrong?"

"All I know is that something feels…off. They hardly talk anymore, and when they do, it's obvious there's tension. I asked them both individually but they swear nothing is wrong."

Nick debated telling him what Terri had seen at *Nonno's* house, but it didn't seem fair to drag her into this. "I don't know, Dad. Have you talked to Rob or Tony?"

"You're close with them. I thought it would be better if you did."

Nick sighed. Unlike most of the rest of the family, Nick had no burning desire to stick his nose into someone else's business. "No offense, but if there is something going on, I don't want to be in the middle of it."

"I'm not asking for much," he said sharply.

"Maybe they told you everything is fine because they feel like, whatever is going on, it's none of your business."

"If it starts to affect this company it is."

"You're the CPA. Is it affecting the company?"

"Not yet, but—"

"Instead of jumping to conclusions, maybe you should just ride it out for a week or two and see what happens. *Nonni* used to tell us that when you and Tony and Demitrio were kids, you had fights all the time."

"This is different," he said.

"Just give it some time, okay? Then if you're still worried, I'll mention it to Rob and Tony."

He nodded grudgingly. "So, how are things with you and Terri?"

"Good." At least he hoped so. She'd been…off lately. She'd been quieter, more closed up than usual. They used to talk on the phone nearly every evening, and the conversations would sometimes last for hours. But lately, they could be sitting in a room together and she barely said two words to him. Sometimes she was so lost in thought, she would seem to forget he was even there.

Maybe it was that she'd been anxious about getting pregnant. Or they just needed time to get used to living together. Whatever it was, he hoped that she would be back to her old self soon. He was beginning to miss his best friend.

"Your mom mentioned that the two of you are planning to start a family soon."

"When did you talk to Mom?"

He hesitated, then said, "At your wedding."

Why did Nick get the feeling that wasn't the only time? And why would he be contacting Nick's mom? Was he harassing her?

Nick made a mental note to ask his mom about it.

"Yes, we're planning on starting a family, but it looks as if it might take a bit longer than we'd hoped."

"So, Terri really isn't pregnant?"

"You shouldn't listen to gossip, Dad. It's beneath you."

He pushed himself to his feet. "If my son would talk to me once in a while, I wouldn't have to."

Maybe, he thought, as his dad stalked out, slamming the door behind him, *if you hadn't been such a rotten husband and father, I would.*

But those words would mean nothing to him, since the great Leonardo Caroselli took no responsibility for his past bad behavior. It was always someone else's fault.

Nick stewed about it for the rest of the day, and began to think that it would ruin his entire evening. When he got home later with the pizza and a bottle of wine, he went searching for Terri, worried that he might discover her curled up in bed crying. Instead, he found her in her office, so focused on her computer screen and the design she was working on, she hadn't even heard him come in.

"Pizza's here," he said.

She turned, surprised to see him, then smiled and said, "Hi, is it seven already?"

In that instant the stress of the day, with his mounting frustration seemed to melt away until all he felt was... happy. And content. But hadn't she always made him feel that way?

He hadn't fully appreciated that until just now.

"I have something to show you," Terri said. "But first…"

She got up from her chair, put her arms around him and hugged him hard. And damn did it feel good to hold her. So good, he didn't want to let go when she backed away.

"What was that for?"

"For being so patient with me, and for being such a good friend. We've gone through some pretty huge changes in the last month. Everything happened so fast, we didn't have much time to prepare ourselves. But at the same time, in the back of my head, I had this idea that we had to hurry, that if I didn't get pregnant right away, if I missed the deadline I set for myself, it would never happen. I think maybe that's why I didn't get pregnant. I was anxious about *everything*."

"I've noticed that, the past week or so, you haven't been yourself. Like you're here, but you aren't really here."

"I know. And I'm sorry I've been so self-absorbed. But from now on, I'm back to being my old self. I promise."

"Good, because I've missed you."

She smiled, then gestured to the calendar on the wall above her desk. "See that highlighted week?"

She had marked the twenty-third to the twenty-seventh in blue. "Yeah."

"Do you know what it is?"

"Um…Christmas vacation?"

"That's the week I'm due to ovulate."

Nick laughed. "Are you serious?"

She smiled and nodded. "That would be a pretty awesome Christmas present, don't you think?"

"It certainly would."

"I think this time it will work."

"And if it doesn't?" He hated to see her get herself all stressed out again.

"If it doesn't, we try again in January. I just want to relax and let things happen naturally."

"And they will," he said. He had a really good feeling about this.

But just when he thought he had everything figured out, thought he knew the plan, a few days later she threw him another curve ball.

Terri's car was parked in the garage when Nick got home from work a few days later, but the apartment was quiet. He looked in the obvious places. Her bedroom, her office, even the laundry room behind the kitchen, but he couldn't find her, or a note explaining where she'd gone. He was about to grab his phone to call her, thinking she may have gone down to the fitness room for a quick workout before dinner, when he swore he heard the sound of running water from the direction of his bedroom.

He walked down the hall to his room and stepped inside. "Terri?"

"In here," she called from his bathroom, and he heard what sounded like the hum of the sauna jets in the tub. Was she cleaning it, maybe?

The bathroom door was open, so he walked in.

Unless she liked to do housework naked and submerged in the water, she was not cleaning anything.

He stopped beside the tub and folded his arms. The water came up to her neck, and with the jets on high, he couldn't see more that a blurry outline of her body, but that was enough to kick his libido into gear. "Something wrong with your tub?"

She smiled up at him. "Nope."

Okay. And she was in his tub because...

"I've been thinking about it, and if we want to get it right this time, if we really want me to get pregnant, maybe we could use a little more practice."

"If you'll recall, I actually suggested that we practice first. You said no."

"I guess I was wrong."

Though it would be all too easy to pretend that he believed her just to get laid, they were both better than that.

"That's an interesting theory. Now, you want to drop the bull and tell me why you're *really* here?"

Terri should have known that Nick would call her out, that he would demand total honesty from her. And as annoying as it could be at times, he kept her honest.

"It's not like you to play games," he said, looking disappointed in her. "If after twenty years you can't be honest with me—"

"I miss you," she blurted out, hating how vulnerable the words made her feel. "I know I'm not supposed to, that we're just friends unless I'm ovulating, but I can't help it."

"Are you saying that you want a sexual relationship outside of baby-making?"

Honestly, it was all she could think about lately, and she was tired of fighting it, tired of feeling as if something was missing. But maybe he didn't feel that same way. "If you think it's a bad idea—"

"I didn't say that." He shrugged out of his suit jacket and hung it on the hook next to the shower stall.

"I know it wasn't part of the plan," she said. "But I've begun to think that the two of us going nine months without any sex is a slightly unrealistic goal. I like sex, and we do it really well together, so why not?"

"You don't think it will complicate things?"

"Why would it? We both want the same thing—to have a baby without getting tied down."

He closed the lid on the toilet and sat. "I thought you were still looking for Mr. Right eventually."

"Instead of trying to find him, I think I may just sit back, relax and let him find me. There's no rush."

"So what happens with us after the baby is born?"

"We get divorced, like we planned."

"And we start seeing other people?"

She shrugged. "I don't see why not."

He looked skeptical. "It wouldn't hurt your feelings, or make you jealous to see me with someone else?"

"I've seen you with lots of women and it never bothered me before." At least, not enough to impact their friendship. Sure, it might be a little strange at first, but they would adjust. Hell, for all she knew, they could be completely sick of each other by then. Going back to a platonic friendship might be a huge relief for them both.

But considering how long it was taking Nick to respond, maybe he didn't think it was such a hot idea. He had been pretty hands-off lately, not so touchy-feely as before. Even when they slept together in his bed the other night, he hadn't put the moves on her. Maybe he was only interested in sleeping with her when they were trying to make the baby.

He rested his elbows on his knees, his hands folded under his chin. He was deep in thought, as if maybe he was trying to come up with some way to let her down easy.

A knot formed in her stomach, and she started to get the distinct impression she had just made a big ass of herself. But it was too late to back out now. Not without making herself look like an even *bigger* ass. The one time she took a chance and put herself out there on a limb—

"You're sure about this?" Nick said.

She nodded, feeling a slight glimmer of hope.

"*Really* sure?"

"Really sure."

"Because not touching you the past ten days has been hell on earth. So you can't just sleep with me once, then change your mind again. Either you're in or you're out. There's no middle ground. Agreed?"

Whoa. "Agreed."

"Now that we have that settled," he said, grinning and tugging his tie loose, "scoot over."

Thirteen

"Earth to Nick!"

Nick's attention jerked from the notepad he hadn't even realized he'd been doodling on. Everyone at the conference room table—his dad, his uncles, plus Rob, Tony and Elana—was looking at him.

"Sorry, what?"

"Have you heard anything we've said?" his dad snapped, as if Nick were a stubborn child and not a capable adult. Well, maybe not so capable right now, but that really wasn't Nick's fault.

"Currently sales for the quarter are down," Nick said, regurgitating the only snippet of the conversation he'd heard so far.

"Is that it? You didn't hear anything else?"

"Sorry, I didn't get much sleep last night."

"Have you tried a sleeping pill?"

"Leo, he's still a newlywed," Demitrio said, winking at Nick. "He's not supposed to sleep."

Yeah, and Terri had kept him up particularly late. They made love after the nightly news, then at 2:00 a.m. he woke to find her buried under the covers doing some pretty amazing things with her mouth. But starting today they had to abstain until she ovulated. And though he never thought he would catch himself thinking it, he was ready for a break.

Since the first day of their honeymoon, the sex had been great, but this past week she had been *insatiable*. They made love in the morning, either in bed or in the shower, and if he had no meeting scheduled for lunch he would come home for a quickie. Yesterday he'd asked her to bring him a report he'd left on his home office desk, and when she got there, she'd had that look in her eye. Then she locked his office door and he knew he was in trouble.

They did it some evenings right when he got home from work, and always when they got into bed at night. They had done it in the tub, on the sofa, in his office chair and about a dozen other places. It seemed as if every time he turned around, she was poised to jump him.

Not that he was complaining. But, *damn*, he was getting tired.

"We're considering bringing in a consultant," Demitrio told him. "Someone to view our line with a fresh set of eyes. Someone who could help us update our marketing without losing the essence of who we are as a company."

"Who are we thinking of?" Nick asked, noticing that Rob, as marketing director, did not look happy.

"Her name is Caroline Taylor. She's based on the West Coast, and she comes highly recommended. She's not cheap, though."

"Which is why I think we're wasting our money and our time," Rob said.

Nick was sure it had more to do with Rob's bruised ego. If they brought in another chocolatier to develop new products, Nick would be insulted, too.

"Son, this in no way reflects on your job performance," Demitrio said. "It's quite common for companies to bring in outside consultants. We've been talking about a fresh look for the company, and I believe the time is now."

Rob clearly wasn't happy about it, but he didn't argue, either.

"I take it we've contacted her already," Nick said. Undoubtedly, someone had mentioned this, but he'd missed it.

"Yes, and we got lucky," Demitrio said. "She's typically booked up for months, and sometimes years in advance, but the company she was supposed to start with in January went bankrupt. She's all ours if we want her. And I have to give her an answer by the end of the week."

Everyone, except Rob, of course, thought it was a good idea.

"Great!" Demitrio said. "We wanted to run it past everyone first, and the board will make a final decision tomorrow."

Uncle Tony was up and out the door before anyone else had a chance to stand up. Though Nick tuned out most of the meeting, during the parts he did catch, his uncle Tony hadn't said a word. Maybe his dad was right, and there was something going on between his uncles.

Nick knew that his uncle Tony had always followed the rules. He went to the right schools, graduating with honors and worked his way up through the ranks. Uncle Demitrio, on the other hand, had been a hell-raiser, uninterested in the family business, in and out of trouble with the law until he joined the army. Nick had heard his dad mention that while everyone else in the family had to earn their position, Demitrio had everything handed to him. Maybe that was causing hard feelings between Tony and Demitrio. But then, how did Aunt Sarah factor into that?

As Nick walked back to his office, Rob caught up with him in the hall. "So, any baby news to report?"

"First try was a bust."

"I'm sorry. How did she take it?"

"Not well at first, but she's okay now. We're just going to take it one cycle at time."

"Besides work, Tony and I haven't been seeing much of you lately."

"That's married life, I guess." Nick stopped in front of his office door and leaned on the jamb. "Maybe after Christmas we can all go out. Maybe even for New Year's."

"We could do that."

He was quiet for several seconds, and Nick asked, "Something on your mind, Rob?"

"I feel as if I owe you an apology."

"For what?"

"When you told us you were marrying Terri, instead of congratulating you, we accused you of doing something underhanded."

"And threatened to kick my ass, if I recall correctly."

"And it was a lousy thing for us to do. A person just has to see you two together to know that you really love each other, and not only that, it's obvious you're best friends. Which I think is really cool. If only it could be that way for everyone, there would never be another divorce. You really don't know how lucky you are to have her."

"Believe me, I know." And the more he thought of divorcing Terri, the less he liked the idea. He was beginning to wonder if the feelings of love that he'd been having for her were the romantic kind. And he had the distinct feeling that she was wondering the same thing. In their entire relationship he had never felt so close, so…connected. Not to her, and not to anyone else for that matter.

Most of his relationships—the semi-serious ones—rarely lasted much more than a month or two before he started to feel restless and smothered. With Terri, it felt as if there weren't enough hours in the day to spend with her. But at some point, they were going to have to make a decision. In his mind, he was pretty sure the decision was already made.

"Did you get her a Christmas present yet?"

"Not yet," Nick said. "But I have something in mind."

"First Christmas as a married couple. It better be special."

"Oh, it will be," he said, although he had no clue how he was going to wrap it.

On the Saturday before Christmas, which was two days before she was due to ovulate again—yeah, they were both climbing the walls in anticipation—Nick and Terri braved the crowds and four inches of freshly fallen snow to finish up their holiday shopping. They had both been so busy with work, they hadn't had time to get a tree. It seemed silly to go all-out so late in the season, so they picked up a pre-lit, battery-operated tabletop version to set on the coffee table.

She bent and fluffed the artificial branches into what sort of resembled a real tree—a real, *small* tree—switched the lights on then sat back on her heels to admire her work. "Not too shabby."

"What are we going to hang on it?"

She sat beside him on the sofa. "Your mom has a box of stuff that's made for a small tree. She put it aside for us."

"You want me to go pick it up?"

"Would you mind?"

"We're supposed to get another six inches tonight. If we wait, we may not get the ornaments until after Christmas."

"In that case you should probably go."

"Did you want to come with me?"

She sighed. "I can't. I have about fifty gifts to wrap. And if I recall correctly, you were going to help."

"You choose. Decorations or wrapping, which would you prefer?"

She though about that for a second, then said, "Decorations, I guess."

He pushed himself off the sofa. "I'd better go now, before the snow starts again."

She followed him to the door and watched as he put on his coat and checked his pockets for his wallet and keys. "Anything else you need me to pick up while I'm out?"

"Dinner?"

"You don't want to fix something?" He'd been making her watch him cook every night, yet she hadn't tested out what she'd been learning.

"Would you prefer a microwave frozen dinner, or burnt grilled cheese and tomato soup?"

"Fine, I'll pick up dinner. Thai okay?"

"Sounds delicious."

She kissed him goodbye. What shouldn't have been more that a quick peck, lingered. Then her arms went around his neck and her tongue was in his mouth, as one of her legs slid between his.

"Hey!" he said, pulling away. "That was an illegal move, lady. Two more days."

She flashed him a wicked smile. "Just keeping you on your toes."

He opened the door to leave, looking at their pathetic excuse for a tree. "Are you sure you don't mind having this tiny fake thing? You always get a real tree."

"So we'll get a real one next year," she said. "Drive safe."

Nick was in the elevator, on his way down to his car before Terri's words finally sank in.

So we'll get a real one next year....

Did that mean she was planning on them having a next year? That she thought they would still be married? Did she *want* to stay married? He'd been considering bringing up the subject, just to test the waters, but he hadn't yet figured out what he wanted to say. Was this it, handed to him on a silver platter?

And now that he knew she was thinking about it, too, how did he feel?

Nick got in his car and sat there for several minutes, thinking about what it would mean to both of them to make this a real marriage. To spend the rest of their lives together.

That was a really long time.

He drove to his mom's condo on autopilot, but as he turned the wheel to park in the driveway, he saw it was already occupied. *By his dad's car.*

Aw, hell, this couldn't be good.

Hackles up, Nick hopped out of his Mercedes and jogged through an inch of fresh snow to the door. He rang the bell, and when she didn't answer, he knocked briskly. Still no answer.

This was *really* not good.

He used his key and opened the door. He stepped inside, expecting to hear shouting, or furniture crashing. Instead, he heard the faint sound of a radio playing a classic rock song—which his mother favored—then a muffled moan of pain, all coming from the back of the condo.

Oh, hell, they've gone and done it now, he thought, picturing one of them with an actual hatchet in their back. Or possibly missing a limb or, God forbid, some other protruding part.

He rushed down the hall, tracking snow all the way. Realizing the noise was coming from his mom's bedroom, he burst through the partially closed door. And when he got an eyeful of his dad's bare rear end, he realized that no one was feeling any pain. At least, nothing they didn't want to feel.

Nick cursed and covered his eyes, realizing that he'd just walked in on every child's worst nightmare—his parents in bed doing it.

He heard the rustle of the covers and then his mom said, "Nick, what on earth are you doing here?"

He dared move his hand, relieved to find that they had covered themselves, and were in a less compromising position.

"What am *I* doing here? What is *he* doing here? And why in God's name were you…" He couldn't even say the words. He knew the memory of the whole gruesome scene would be eternally burned in his memory, and would haunt him until the day he died. "What the hell is going on?"

"What do you think is going on?" his mom asked, sounding infuriatingly reasonable. "We're having sex."

Ugh, it was bad enough to see it, but to have verbal confirmation was just too much. "You can't do this."

"Obviously, we can," his dad said, looking amused.

"Nicky, we're two single, consenting adults. We can do whatever we want. Within the boundaries of the law," she said, giving Nick's dad a wink.

Nick sniffed, catching just a hint of something that had been burning…. "What the… Have you been smoking *marijuana?*"

"Like you never have," his mom said. "Besides, it's medicinal, for your father's back."

The nightmare just kept getting worse. "You *hate* each other."

"We've certainly had our differences, I won't deny that, but we don't *hate* each other. And though we may have had a bad marriage, we had a good sex life."

He always knew that his mom's mother-earth, hippie-child attitude would come back to bite him. And speaking of that, were those teeth marks on his dad's left biceps…?

He closed his eyes, wishing the vision away.

"Why don't you put on the kettle for tea," his mother said. "We'll be out in a few minutes."

"Sure," Nick said, hoping they weren't planning to finish what they started.

He headed to the kitchen, shrugging out of his coat and draping it across a chair. Then he pulled out his cell phone and dialed Jess's number. When she answered, he could hear the kids screaming in the background, and Jess sounded more than a little exasperated. "What's up?" she shouted over the noise.

"I need to talk to you," he said, keeping his voice low so his parents wouldn't hear.

"What?" she shouted. "You need what?" She paused then said, "Hold on, lemme go somewhere quieter."

While he waited, Nick filled the kettle and set the burner on high. The screaming on the other end of the line faded, and Jess said, "Okay, now I can talk."

"Where did you go?"

"Front hall closet, so it's only a matter of time before they find me or I run out of oxygen."

"I just walked in on Mom and Dad doing it. And they were smoking pot."

She was silent for a several seconds, then said, "Together?"

"Yes, together."

"How did you manage that?"

He explained everything, expecting her to express the same horror he was experiencing. Instead, she started to laugh.

Irritated, he said, "It's not funny. It was...*horrifying*."

"No. It's pretty funny."

"I think you're missing the point. Mom and Dad are *sleeping* together."

"No, I got that. I'm just not sure why you're so freaked out. Would you rather have walked in on Dad chopping Mom into little pieces?"

"No, but...they hate each other."

"All evidence to the contrary. And you should be happy that they're getting along."

"And if he hurts her again?"

"Do you really think she was the only one who was hurt when they divorced?"

That's the way Nick remembered it, but before he could say so, his dad walked into the kitchen.

"I have to go," Nick told Jess. "I'll call you later." He hung up and asked, "Where is Mom?"

"You mother is getting dressed."

Nick's dad walked past him to the sink, pulled down a glass from the cupboard and filled it with tap water. He seemed to know his way around pretty well, which led Nick to believe that this wasn't the first time he'd been here. How long had this thing been going on?

"What the hell do you think you're doing?" he asked his dad.

"Getting a glass of water," he said, taking a swallow. "Would you like one?"

"You know what I mean. After what you did to Mom, what you did to me and the girls, you have no right."

He dumped the rest of the water down the drain, set the glass in the sink then turned to Nick and said, "You're twenty-nine years old, son. Don't you think it's time you grew up?"

The words struck Nick like a slap in the face, rendering him speechless.

"I realize I wasn't the greatest father and I was a pretty lousy husband, but you've been holding this grudge for twenty years. Enough already. Let it go. Everyone else has."

Nick was at a loss. Anything he could say at this point would just come off as immature and petty.

The kettle began to howl as his mom walked into the kitchen, dressed in hot-pink workout gear. "Who would like a cup of tea?" she asked, sounding infuriatingly cheerful. Who wouldn't be cheerful after an afternoon of sex, drugs and rock 'n' roll?

"Rain check," his dad said, then gave Nick's mom a kiss. It was disturbing to watch, but almost…natural in a weird way. They seemed like two people who were perfectly comfortable with each other, and happy to be so.

When the hell had that happened? And how had he missed it?

Fourteen

"Tea?" his mom asked Nick after his dad left.

"Sure," he said when what he really needed was a stiff drink.

"Have a seat," she said, gesturing to the kitchen table. He sat down and watched as she got out the sugar and cream and placed them on the table. When the tea was ready, she set a cup in front of him, then sat down across from him with her own. "So, to what do I owe this unexpected visit?"

For a minute he couldn't remember why he was there, then he remembered. "Decorations for our ugly little tree."

"Well, for future reference, if you ring the bell and I don't answer, come back later."

Yeah, he'd learned that lesson the hard way. "I'm sorry. It was inappropriate of me to barge in like that. But when I saw Dad's car, I was concerned."

"About what? You didn't honestly believe that I was in some sort of danger? That your father would hurt me?"

When she said it that way, it did sound sort of stupid. "I guess I didn't know what to think. Everything has gotten so...jumbled up lately. I don't know what to think about anything anymore."

"Oh, honey." She reached out to cover his hand with her own. "Are you and Terri having problems?"

"Not exactly."

She gave his hand a firm squeeze. "Take it from someone who knows. Marriage is tough. You have to keep the lines of communication open. You have to really work at it."

"And if it's going *too* well?"

Confused, she said, "*Too* well?"

He should shut his mouth now, since she was never supposed to know about this, but who else could he talk to?

"Despite what everyone believes, my marriage to Terri was never supposed to last."

She blinked. "I don't understand."

"Terri wanted a baby, and she was going to use a donor."

"I know. She and I discussed it."

"Well, the gist of it was, why use a donor and not be sure what she was getting, when she could use someone she knew? Specifically me. That way the baby would have lots of family, and if something were ever to happen to Terri, she knows he will be well taken care of."

He didn't dare tell her about the ten million. He could live with the entire family knowing about their baby arrangement, but if his mom blabbed about *Nonno*'s offer, he was a dead man.

"Well," she said stiffly. "It sounds as if you have it all figured out."

"You're angry?"

"No... Yes." She stood so fast her chair almost fell over backward. It teetered on two legs, then landed with a thunk upright.

"Mom—"

"I'm mad. I'm disappointed." She paced back and forth behind him, her puny little hands balled up, as if she might haul off and pop him one. Which would probably hurt her more than it would hurt him. "How could you lie to your family that way?"

"It's not as if I could tell everyone the truth."

That's when he felt it, a firm crack against the back of his head so hard he could swear he heard his brain rattle. She must have been channeling *Nonni* for that one.

"Jeez, Mom." He rubbed the still-stinging part of his head.

His mom sat back down, looking much calmer. "I feel better now."

"I'm sorry, okay? We didn't do it to hurt anyone. You know how much Terri wanted a baby. And you've said a million times that you love her like a daughter. Would you prefer her baby be your grandchild or the product of some random sperm donor?"

"But you two seem so happy, so in love. You can't fake that."

"Maybe we weren't."

"You love her?"

"I think I do."

"And how does Terri feel?"

"That you can never depend on anyone, because eventually they'll let you down."

She sucked in a quiet breath. "Oh, that's not good. But I'm not surprised. She's been hurt a lot."

"But since she said it, things have been really great. And today she was making plans for next Christmas, so I'm thinking maybe that means she wants to stay married, too. I just want to be sure of my own feelings before I make a move, because two years from now, I don't want to wake up one day and realize I've made a terrible mistake. Because I will have lost my wife *and* my best friend."

"Not all marriages go bad, Nicky."

"Mom, you can't deny that our family hasn't exactly had an impressive track record when it comes to successful marriages. You and Dad were a disaster. Jess is miserable."

"There's a reason for that, you know."

"A Caroselli family curse?"

"Nicky, what you have to understand is that your dad and I, we were never friends. When it came to sexual compatibility, we were off the charts, but you can't base a marriage on sex. It just doesn't work. At least, not long past the honeymoon. And your sister, she was so determined to prove that she was different than her parents, that she would never make the same mistakes, she rushed into a relationship before she was ready. And when it started to go south, she didn't have the skills to know how to fix it. Which unfortunately, is partly my fault. I wasn't much of a role model. It's taken me until very recently to get my head together and realize what a real relationship should be. And you know who helped me?"

He shook his head.

"You and Terri."

"Seriously?"

"Maybe you two don't see what everyone else does, but you really are perfectly matched."

"Maybe this is a stupid question, but if your marriage was that bad, and you were that unhappy, why have kids?"

"Because you think it will change things, bring you closer together. And it does for a while. Which is why, when things get bad again, you have another baby, and then another."

Which explained why Jess had four kids of her own, he supposed. "So what you're saying is, you only had us kids to save your marriage?"

"Of course not. I was thrilled when I found out I was pregnant with all three of you. You kids were the light of my life, and sometimes the only thing that kept me going, when I thought I couldn't take another second of being miserable." She reached up, touched his cheek. "You and your sisters always made me happy."

"If you were so miserable, why did you stay married for so long?"

"I came from a broken home, and I wanted better for you. I thought that if I couldn't be happy, the least I could do was give you kids a stable home with two parents."

"Our home was anything but stable, Mom."

She sighed. "I know. But I had to try. And you will never know how sorry I am for what I put you kids through. And so is your father. We were both doing the best we could, or what we thought was best."

"And what you two are doing now, is that for the best, too?"

She shrugged. "All I know is, we have fun together. We talk and we laugh, and he seems to understand me in a way no one else ever has. And the sex—"

Nick held up a hand to stop her. "TMI, Mom."

She grinned. "The point is, right now, he makes me happy. Maybe it will last, maybe it won't. Maybe we both just needed to grow up. Who knows? What I do know is that after all this time, we've finally become friends. With you and Terri, it's different. You're already friends. What you have to decide now is if you love her."

"We've been friends for twenty years. Of course I love her."

"But are you *in love* with her?"

He shrugged. "I guess I don't know the difference."

She looked at him like he was a moron. And she was probably right. Maybe what he needed was another good hard whack in the head.

"Okay, let me ask you this. Who is the first person you think of in the morning when you wake up?"

That was easy. "Terri."

"And when you're not with her, how often do you think about her?"

Lately, too many times to count. "If there was a way I could be with her twenty-four hours a day, I would do it."

"Now, think about when you're with her and find a single word to describe how she makes you feel."

He thought that would be a tough one, since she made him feel so many things lately. But with barely any thought, the perfect word came to him. "Complete," he said. "When I'm with her I feel complete."

"And has anyone else ever made you feel that way?"

"Never," he admitted. Not even close.

"Now, imagine her with someone else."

There was no one else good enough for her. No one who knew her the way he did. Who could ever love her as much…

The answer must have been written all over his face, because his mom smiled. "What do you think that means, Nicky?"

What it meant was, he didn't just love Terri, he was *in* love with her. Looking back, there was hardly a time when he hadn't been. He sighed and shook his head at the depth of his own stupidity. "I am such an idiot."

His mom patted his hand. "When it comes to relationships, most men are, sweetheart."

"What if Terri is still afraid to trust me? How do I convince Terri that I love her, and that I won't let her down? How do I make her trust me?"

She shrugged. "It may take some sort of grand gesture to convince her. But if you know her as well as I think you do, you'll figure it out."

When it came to things like grand gestures, he was clueless. He could barely get his own head straight, and now he was supposed to figure her out, too?

"And while you're at it," his mom said. "Maybe you could cut your dad a little slack. Everyone makes mistakes."

"Some more than others."

"And goodness knows you can hold a grudge. But haven't you punished him enough? Couldn't you at least *try* to let him make amends? Would you do it for me?"

Maybe Nick had been a bit bullheaded—a trait he had inherited from his father, of course—but to be honest, he was tired of carrying around this pent-up animosity. After all his parents had been through, if she could forgive him, shouldn't he at least make an attempt?

"I'll try," he told her.

His mom smiled. "Thank you."

"I'm sorry I barged in on you like that," he said.

"Well, considering the look on your face, it was much more traumatic for you than it was for your father and me."

No kidding.

When he left his mom's condo, he went straight home, still completely clueless as to what he would say to Terri.

With any luck, he would have some sort of epiphany, and the right words would just come to him. That was bound to happen at least once in a man's life, right?

When Nick got home, Terri was sitting on the living room floor amid a jumble of wrapping paper, ribbon and bows.

"I'm home," he said, even though that was pretty obvious, as he was standing right there. He was off to a champion start.

She just looked at him and smiled and said, "How are the roads?"

"Getting bad," he said. "How's the wrapping?"

"I've been doing this every year for over twenty years now, and I still manage to suck at it."

He reviewed the pile of presents she'd already finished, and it did sort of look as if a five-year-old had done them.

"Plus my knees are about to pop." She pushed herself to her feet and watched him expectantly. "So where is it?"

He hung up his coat. "Where is what?"

"The decorations."

"Oh, crap." He'd been so rattled when he left his mom's he'd forgotten to grab the box.

"You drove all the way to you mom's and *forgot* them?"

"I'm sorry."

"I don't suppose you picked up dinner, either."

Dammit! "No, I forgot that, too. But I have a very good excuse. I walked in on my parents having sex."

Her eyes went wide, and she said, *"Together?"*

He repeated the story to her, and by the end she was laughing so hard tears were rolling down her face.

"It is *not funny,*" he said.

"Yeah," she said, wiping her eyes. "It is."

"I'm traumatized for life. Did I also mention that they were smoking pot?"

"Like you've never done that," she said. She walked into the kitchen and he followed her. "So what are we going to eat? I'm starving."

"We could order in."

"In this weather, it will take forever."

"I could throw together a quick tomato sauce, and serve it over shells. It wouldn't take more than an hour."

"After shopping all day, then living through the horror of seeing your dad's naked ass, do you really think you have the energy?"

Shaking his head in exasperation, he snatched his apron from the broom closet. "Get me two cans of crushed tomatoes and a can of tomato paste from the pantry."

He tied the apron on and grabbed the ingredients he needed from the fridge. He chopped onions, celery and garlic, and sautéed it all in a pan with olive oil. When the onions and garlic turned translucent, he stirred in the crushed tomatoes and tomato paste, then added oregano, basil and salt. He ground fresh pepper in next, then added the slightest pinch of thyme, which his *Nonni* had always taught him to use sparingly, warning that too much would overwhelm. Nick had learned a lot in culinary school, but the really valuable things he'd learned from her.

"How do you do that?" Terri asked from the bar stool where she sat watching him. "You don't measure anything. How do you know it's the right amount?"

"I do measure it. Just with my eyes, not a spoon. When you make something as many times as I've made *Nonni's* tomato sauce, a recipe becomes obsolete."

She sighed. "I can't make toast without screwing it up."

"It's just a matter of following the directions and using good judgment."

"Well, there you go, I have terrible judgment."

"You married me," he said, hoping to break the ice. Maybe she would say it had been the best decision of her life.

She smiled at him and said, "I rest my case."

He laughed in spite of himself. He set the burner on medium and took off his apron. "So, I was thinking maybe we could—"

His cell phone buzzed in his pants pocket, startling him. Then it started to ring. He pulled it out and saw that it was Rob. "Hold on a minute, Terri.

"Hey, Rob," he answered.

"Hey, have you got a minute?"

"Um, I'm making dinner."

"It'll just take a minute."

"Okay, sure, what's up?"

"Something kind of weird happened yesterday, and I'm really not sure what to think. I thought maybe your dad said something to you about it."

"You know me and my dad, always chatting."

"I know it's a long shot, but I thought maybe he mentioned it."

"Mentioned what?"

"What's going on between my dad and Uncle Tony."

"Actually he did mention it, but only to ask if I knew what was going on. Which I don't. He wanted me to ask you and Tony Junior if you knew anything."

"All I know is that I stopped by my parents' house tonight and Uncle Tony's Beemer was there. I heard shouting from inside, and when my mom answered the door, she looked as if she'd been crying, and Uncle Tony looked pissed. He left just a few minutes after I got there. When I asked what happened, my parents wouldn't talk about it."

"What about Tony? Have you talked to him?"

"A few minutes ago. He didn't have a clue what I was talking about."

He considered mentioning what Terri saw on Thanksgiving, and that whatever it was, Aunt Sarah was involved, too, but he was a little fuzzy on the details. Besides, it wouldn't be fair to bring Terri into this without first asking her if it was okay.

"I'll ask around and see what I can come up with, but I'm sure it's nothing to worry about," he said, even though that was the opposite of what he was actually thinking. Something was up, and he had the feeling it was bad.

Fifteen

"Everything okay?" Terri asked when Nick hung up, but she could tell by the look on his face that something was wrong.

"I'm not sure. According to my father and Rob, there's some sort of friction between Uncle Demitrio and Uncle Tony. Didn't you say that you heard Uncle Demitrio and Aunt Sarah fighting at *Nonno's*?"

He *remembered* that? She wondered what else he recalled from that night. "I don't know if I would call it *fighting,* but it seemed…heated. But like you said, they used to date, so maybe there are still hard feelings."

"Why now, after thirty-some years?"

She shrugged. This was not a can of worms she wanted to be responsible for opening.

"Do you recall what they were fighting about?"

"I didn't hear the whole conversation, just bits and pieces."

"Like what?"

"Something about telling someone something."

"That's vague."

She shrugged. "She said she didn't want to, and then they walked downstairs."

"You didn't hear them mention a name?"

"No. It was probably nothing. Honestly, I figured you would have forgotten all about it."

"I remember a lot of things from that night." Something about the way he said it, the way he looked into her eyes, made her heart skip a beat.

"Wh-what do you remember?" she asked, her heart in her throat, unsure if she really wanted to know.

"Bits and pieces."

"Do you remember saying anything to me?"

"If I recall, I said a lot of things to you. To what specifically were you referring?"

He wanted her to tell him, so he clearly *didn't* remember. She felt an odd mix of relief, and disappointment. "Never mind."

"Was it when I commented on the stuffing?" he asked. "Or when I expressed my unrequited and undying love for you?"

He said it so calmly, so matter-of-factly, that for several seconds words escaped her. She couldn't even breathe. Then she realized that he was just teasing her. She refused to feel disappointed. "I want you to know that you shouldn't feel weird or uncomfortable for saying it."

"I don't."

"All that stuff about you wishing other girls were me. I know you didn't mean it."

"What makes you think I didn't mean it?"

"Because…" She paused, unsure of what to say next, because he had to be messing with her. It was the only explanation. "Nick, come on. You were completely hammered."

"Just because I was drunk doesn't mean I didn't know what I was saying or mean what I said. In fact, that's probably the most honest I've ever been with you. And with myself for that matter."

Suddenly she was having a tough time pulling in a full breath again, and the room pitched so violently she clutched the counter to keep from falling over.

Nick loved her? *Love* loved her? And didn't she want that?

It was one thing to fantasize about it, but she was totally unprepared to actually hear him say the words.

"Besides," he said. "I'm not drunk now. And I still feel the same way, so I guess it must be true."

A small part of her wanted to jump for joy, while another part—a much bigger part—was having a full-blown panic attack.

Slow, shallow breaths. In and out.

What was *wrong* with her? This was a good thing, right? Shouldn't she be happy? A rich, handsome man who just happened to be her best friend in the world love-loved her. Shouldn't she be *thrilled?*

She should, but why wasn't she? Why instead was every fiber of her being screaming at her to run?

"Terri, are you okay?" Nick looked as if he were getting his first inkling that something was off. Specifically, her.

"I'm just a little surprised," she said. "I mean, this definitely was not a part of the plan."

"Plans change."

Not this one.

He sat beside her and took her hands. "Look, I know you're scared."

She pulled her hands free. "It's not that."

"Then what is it?"

"You don't want to be married. You've said it a million times."

"I was wrong."

"Just like that, you changed your mind?"

"Pretty much."

"And how do I know you aren't going to change it back? That five years from now you won't get restless or bored? How do I know you won't die?"

"Okay, Terri," he said calmly, as if he were speaking to a child. "Now you're being ridiculous."

"Am I? Have you forgotten that you're talking to a woman whose parents have both died? Like you said, they probably didn't want to die. I'm guessing they didn't plan on it, either. But they still did."

"I never meant to imply that I'm not going to die. Everyone dies eventually. And, of course, I'm hoping my death occurs later rather than sooner."

"Why are you doing this now? Everything was going so well."

"That's why I'm doing it. After what you said about Christmas, I figured you wanted this, too."

"What did I say about Christmas?"

"That next year we would get a real tree. Which I took to mean that there would be a next year for us, that you're planning for the future."

How could a few innocent words get so dangerously misconstrued? "That wasn't what I meant."

"So what did you mean?"

"I don't know!" She wished he would stop pushing and give her a minute to organize her thoughts. "There was no hidden agenda, they were just words."

"Terri, I am in love with you. I know what I want, and

that isn't going to change. Not a year from now, not five years from now, not a hundred. As long as I am alive, I'm going to want you."

"I want you, too," she said softly. "But I just don't know if I'm ready for this. If you could give me a little time—"

"How much time? A year, two years? Twenty years? Because that's how long it's taken us to get this far. You can't live your life in fear of what might happen."

"This isn't going to work."

"What isn't going to work?"

"The marriage, the baby, none of it. It's not fair to either of us. You want something from me that I just can't give, Nick."

For a minute he didn't say anything. He just sat there staring at the wall. Finally, he said, "You know what I could never figure out? You're beautiful and intelligent, yet you insisted on dating jerks and losers. Men that I— and pretty much everyone else—knew were all wrong for you. And now I realize that was the whole point. Because for all the talking you do about finding Mr. Right, you didn't *want* to find him. You would rather play it safe by getting into a relationship you knew would fail, or one that was just about sex. Because if you didn't care, they couldn't hurt you. But how many people do you think *you* hurt, Terri?"

She bit her lip.

"How many men really cared about you, maybe even loved you, and you just tossed them away? And now you're doing the same thing to me."

He was right, she knew he was, but she couldn't do anything about it. She didn't know how. Those self-defense mechanisms he was referring to were so deep-seated, she didn't know how to be any other way.

"If you could just give me a little more time—"

"Terri, we have been best friends for *twenty* years. If you don't trust me now, you're never going to." He pushed off the bar stool and started to walk away.

"What about the ten million dollars?" she said, only because she wasn't quite ready to let him go. Not yet.

He stopped and turned to her, his face blank, even though she knew he had to be hurting. "There are plenty of other fish in the sea."

He didn't mean it, she knew he didn't, but as he turned and walked away, his words cut deep. If only he could give her a little more time. But he was right, she was damaged goods and he deserved better than her.

When Nick woke the next morning, when he and Terri were supposed to be trying to make a baby, he walked into the spare bedroom to discover that all her clothes were gone. He walked to the kitchen and found "the" note. She said she was sorry and she would be back in a few days to get the rest of her things. Simple, to the point.

And that was it.

Numb, he made a pot of coffee that he never drank, warmed a bagel that he forgot in the toaster, opened a beer that then sat on the coffee table untouched and stared most of the day at a television he never bothered to turn on. And for the first time in years, he did not talk to Terri. He wanted to, though, which surprised him a little. It felt unnatural not telling her about his day, even if all he did was sit around wallowing in self-pity.

On Christmas Eve, at his mom's house, he told everyone she had to flu, knowing that if he told them the truth it would ruin everyone's Christmas. And since this entire mess was his fault, since he was the one who talked Terri into this, and assured her everything would work out great, he deserved to suffer alone. Although he didn't doubt she was suffering, too. And he wished he could take back some of the things he had said to her.

He told himself he wasn't going to miss her, yet caught himself expecting her to be there, because she hadn't missed a holiday with his family in years. Because she had no one else.

He was miserable, but at least he was with people who loved him. She was miserable, too—he didn't doubt for a second that she was—but on top of that, she was alone. Guilt gnawed at him all evening. He hardly slept. By Christmas morning, he knew what he had to do, what he *needed* to do. And yes, what he wanted to do.

From the outside, Terri's condo was the only one that was bare of holiday decorations. It looked so…lonely. A misfit among units draped with twinkling lights and fresh pine wreathes and nativity scenes. They hadn't exactly gone all out at his place, either, but at least they had their scrawny and unadorned little tree that sat for a couple days on the coffee table looking as lonely and pathetic as he felt.

He trudged through two inches of freshly fallen snow to her door and rang the bell. Terri opened it wearing flannel pajamas, due, he had no doubt, to the sub-zero temperature where she kept the thermostat. She was stunned to see him, of course, just as he'd expected she would be. So stunned that for several long seconds she just stared openmouthed at him.

"It's really cold out here," he said, and she snapped into action.

"Sorry, come in."

She held the door for him and he stepped inside. He stomped the snow from his shoes and shrugged out of his coat, surprised to find that it was reasonably warm. "This is nice," he said.

"Nice?" she asked.

"The temperature. It's usually so cold."

"I decided last night that I'm sick of being cold."

It was about time.

"What are you doing here?" she asked as he walked through the foyer into the living room. Her laptop sat open on the coffee table and the television was tuned to what he recognized as some cheesy made-for-television holiday flick she'd forced him to watch a couple years ago.

"I'm picking you up," he said, making himself comfortable on the sofa.

"Picking me up for *what?*"

"Christmas at *Nonno's.*"

"But…"

"You better hurry. You know how he hates it when people are late."

She stared at him, dumbfounded. "I'm sorry, did I miss something?"

"I don't think so. It's Christmas day, and on Christmas day we always go to *Nonno's.*"

"But…the other day…?"

"I'm really sorry about that."

Just when he thought she couldn't look any more confused. "*You're* sorry."

"What I did to you was really unfair. I basically forced you into doing this, assured you repeatedly that everything would be great, and work out exactly according to plan, then I changed my mind and got angry when you were surprised. I tried to make you feel guilty when it was my fault, not yours."

"Nick, you had every right to be mad at me."

"No, I didn't."

"And now you're here to take me to Christmas dinner?"

"Did you honestly think I would let you spend Christmas alone?"

Tears pooled in her eyes, but didn't spill over. "Actually, I sort of thought I deserved it."

"Well, I don't think so. So go get ready."

"So we're just going to be friends again? Like before?"

"If that's my only option. I won't say that I don't love you, because I do. I think I probably always have, even if I was too stupid to realize it. But you're too important to me to let you go, and if friendship is all you want, I'm okay with that."

One minute Terri was standing in front of him looking thoroughly confused, and the next she was sitting in his lap, arms around his neck, hugging him harder than she'd ever hugged him before.

"I love you, Nick."

Now he was the confused one. "Okay, what just happened?"

She sat back on his thighs and laughed. "I don't know. All of a sudden I just…knew."

"That constituted a grand gesture?"

"A what?"

He shook his head. "Never mind."

"I have a confession," she said. "Something I've been wanting to tell you for weeks."

"What?"

"When we lived together, and you brought girls over, I used to wish it was me in the bedroom with you."

"No, you didn't."

"I *did*. I always wondered what it would be like."

"And now that you know?"

She grinned. "I really like being the girl in the bedroom with you. And the idea of another girl being there instead of me…"

"How would you feel?"

"Like ripping out her throat with my bare hands."

He laughed. "Well, you'll never have to, because there's no one else I want there, either. Because despite what I said, those vows meant something to me. And I was meant to say them to you."

She grinned. "Wow, that was so sappy, I don't know if I should laugh or cry."

"Why don't you kiss me instead?"

She did, and then she started to unbutton his shirt.

He caught her hands. "We really don't have time. *Nonno* is expecting us."

"Well, *Nonno* will have to wait. We have business in the bedroom. We're already two days behind schedule."

He'd completely forgotten that she was ovulating. "Well, just a quick one I guess. If you're sure you still want to. We can wait a month."

"I don't want to wait. I know what I want, and besides, aren't you looking forward to all the money?"

"Oh, well, don't even worry about that."

"Why?"

"I told him I didn't want the money anymore."

Her mouth dropped open. "What? *When?*"

"Right after we got back from the honeymoon."

"Why?"

"It just didn't feel right taking it."

"What did *Nonno* say?"

"Not much. I thought he would be really surprised, but it was almost as if he was expecting it."

"But it's ten *million* dollars! You just gave that up?"

"I'm having a child with you because I *want* to, not because I need to."

She cupped his face in her soft hands. "Have I mentioned that I love you?"

He grinned. "Why don't you tell me again?"

"I love you, Nicolas Caroselli."

"What about that perfect man you were looking for? Are you ready to give him up?"

"I don't have to."

"You don't?"

"Heck, no," she said with one of those wicked grins. "I already married him."

* * * * *

COMING NEXT MONTH from Harlequin Desire®
AVAILABLE NOVEMBER 27, 2012

#2197 ONE WINTER'S NIGHT
The Westmorelands
Brenda Jackson

Riley Westmoreland never mixes business with pleasure—until he meets his company's gorgeous new party planner and realizes one night will never be enough.

#2198 A GOLDEN BETRAYAL
The Highest Bidder
Barbara Dunlop

The head of a New York auction house is swept off her feet by the crown prince of a desert kingdom who has accused her of trafficking in stolen goods!

#2199 STAKING HIS CLAIM
Billionaires and Babies
Tessa Radley

She never planned a baby...he doesn't plan to let his baby go. The solution should be simple. But no one told Ella that love is the riskiest business of all....

#2200 BECOMING DANTE
The Dante Legacy
Day Leclaire

Gabe Moretti discovers he's not just a Moretti—he's a secret Dante. Now the burning passion—the Inferno—for Kat Malloy won't be ignored....

#2201 THE SHEIKH'S DESTINY
Desert Knights
Olivia Gates

Marrying Laylah is Rashid's means to the throne. But when she discovers his plot and casts him from her heart, will claiming the throne mean anything if he loses her?

#2202 THE DEEPER THE PASSION...
The Drummond Vow
Jennifer Lewis

When Vicki St. Cyr is forced to ask the man who broke her heart for help in claiming a reward, old passions and long-buried emotions flare.

You can find more information on upcoming Harlequin® titles, free excerpts and more at www.Harlequin.com.

HDCNM1112

REQUEST YOUR FREE BOOKS!
2 FREE NOVELS PLUS 2 FREE GIFTS!

Harlequin®

Desire

ALWAYS POWERFUL, PASSIONATE AND PROVOCATIVE

YES! Please send me 2 FREE Harlequin Desire® novels and my 2 FREE gifts (gifts are worth about $10). After receiving them, if I don't wish to receive any more books, I can return the shipping statement marked "cancel." If I don't cancel, I will receive 6 brand-new novels every month and be billed just $4.30 per book in the U.S. or $4.99 per book in Canada. That's a saving of at least 14% off the cover price! It's quite a bargain! Shipping and handling is just 50¢ per book in the U.S. and 75¢ per book in Canada.* I understand that accepting the 2 free books and gifts places me under no obligation to buy anything. I can always return a shipment and cancel at any time. Even if I never buy another book, the two free books and gifts are mine to keep forever.

225/326 HDN FEF3

Name	(PLEASE PRINT)

Address		Apt. #

City	State/Prov.	Zip/Postal Code

Signature (if under 18, a parent or guardian must sign)

Mail to the **Reader Service:**
IN U.S.A.: P.O. Box 1867, Buffalo, NY 14240-1867
IN CANADA: P.O. Box 609, Fort Erie, Ontario L2A 5X3

Not valid for current subscribers to Harlequin Desire books.

Want to try two free books from another line?
Call 1-800-873-8635 or visit www.ReaderService.com.

* Terms and prices subject to change without notice. Prices do not include applicable taxes. Sales tax applicable in N.Y. Canadian residents will be charged applicable taxes. Offer not valid in Quebec. This offer is limited to one order per household. All orders subject to credit approval. Credit or debit balances in a customer's account(s) may be offset by any other outstanding balance owed by or to the customer. Please allow 4 to 6 weeks for delivery. Offer available while quantities last.

Your Privacy—The Reader Service is committed to protecting your privacy. Our Privacy Policy is available online at www.ReaderService.com or upon request from the Reader Service.

We make a portion of our mailing list available to reputable third parties that offer products we believe may interest you. If you prefer that we not exchange your name with third parties, or if you wish to clarify or modify your communication preferences, please visit us at www.ReaderService.com/consumerschoice or write to us at Reader Service Preference Service, P.O. Box 9062, Buffalo, NY 14269. Include your complete name and address.

HDES11B

Harlequin® Desire is proud to present

ONE WINTER'S NIGHT

by New York Times *bestselling author*

Brenda Jackson

Alpha Blake tightened her coat around her. Not only would she be late for her appointment with Riley Westmoreland, but because of her flat tire they would have to change the location of the meeting and Mr. Westmoreland would be the one driving her there. This was totally embarrassing, when she had been trying to make a good impression.

She turned up the heat in her car. Even with a steady stream of hot air coming in through the car vents, she still felt cold, too cold, and wondered if she would ever get used to the Denver weather. Of course, it was too late to think about that now. It was her first winter here, and she didn't have any choice but to grin and bear it. When she'd moved, she'd felt that getting as far away from Daytona Beach as she could was essential to her peace of mind. But who in her right mind would prefer blistering-cold Denver to sunny Daytona Beach? Only a person wanting to start a new life and put a painful past behind her.

Her attention was snagged by an SUV that pulled off the road and parked in front of her. The door swung open and long denim-clad, boot-wearing legs appeared before a man stepped out of the truck. She met his gaze through the windshield and forgot to breathe. Walking toward her car was a man who was so dangerously masculine, so heart-stoppingly virile, that her brain went momentarily numb.

He was tall, and the Stetson on his head made him appear taller. But his height was secondary to the sharp handsomeness of his features.

Her gaze slid all over him as he moved his long limbs toward her vehicle in a walk that was so agile and self-assured, she envied the confidence he exuded with every step. Her breasts suddenly peaked, and she could actually feel blood rushing through her veins.

She didn't have to guess who this man was.

He was Riley Westmoreland.

Find out if Riley and Alpha mix business with pleasure in

ONE WINTER'S NIGHT

by Brenda Jackson

Available December 2012

Only from Harlequin® Desire

HARLEQUIN®

SPECIAL EDITION

Life, Love and Family

NEW YORK TIMES BESTSELLING AUTHOR

DIANA PALMER

brings you a brand-new Western romance
featuring characters that readers have come to
love—the Brannt family from Harlequin HQN's
bestselling book *WYOMING TOUGH*.

Cort Brannt, Texas rancher through and through,
is about to unexpectedly get lassoed by love!

THE RANCHER

Available November 13 wherever books are sold!

Also available as a 2-in-1
THE RANCHER & HEART OF STONE

HSE65709DP